The Way of the Kings

The Way of the Kings

André Malraux

Translated by Howard Curtis

ET REMOTISSIMA PROPE

Modern Voices

Modern Voices
Published by Hesperus Press Limited
4 Rickett Street, London SW6 1RU
www.hesperuspress.com

The Way of the Kings first published in French as *La Voie royale* in 1930
La Voie royale © Éditions Bernard Grasset, 1930.
First published by Hesperus Press Limited, 2005

Introduction and English language translation © Howard Curtis, 2005
Foreword © Rachel Seiffert, 2005

Designed and typeset by Fraser Muggeridge
Printed in Jordan by the Jordan National Press

ISBN: 1-84391-406-9

Contents

Foreword

I knew of Malraux only by political reputation: that he had flown fighters for the Republicans in Spain, and had escaped the Gestapo to join the Resistance. He was for me a romantic figure, a passionate anti-fascist with wind-ruffled hair and a filterless cigarette permanently jammed into the corner of his mouth. That he was also a novelist had somehow passed me by, and so I was grateful for this opportunity to read him.

The Way of the Kings is difficult to define. Set largely in French Indochina, following the exploits of two white men, a Frenchman and a Dane, it could be described as a critique of the European imperial drive, or an examination of male friendship, or a treatise on sexuality and power. Any of the above would do, I suppose, but all such interpretations seem dry and pale beside the novel itself. While Malraux's philosophical preoccupations are undeniably present, what lasts beyond the reading is the powerful, passionate writing.

In Claude, Malraux gives us a sceptical protagonist through whom to see the French authorities. Claude shows a wry contempt for white colonial society, dismissing it as pompous, suffocating, peopled by those 'whose slicked-down hair signified their distinction.' Perken stands apart from this crowd, the subject of intense gossip and speculation, an enigmatic *heimatlos* adventurer, at once useful to the authorities and an embarrassment to them. Claude is drawn to Perken's utter disregard for social status, seduced by his notion that experience, whether good or bad, is the only goal worth pursuing. Crucially, neither man can bear the compromises which conventional European society requires.

Each begins the novel with a quest, a borderline obsession. Claude for the statues and bas-reliefs of the Siamese temples built along the ancient Way of the Kings, Perken for an errant former colleague, Grabot, who has lost himself somewhere in the vast rainforest between Laos, Cambodia and Thailand. In the course of the narrative, both men will abandon these original objects, but never the insistent desire which underpinned their pursuit. It is as though the desire preceded the obsession and will always find new objects to fuel it, if only each man will continue to 'throw his imagination' as if 'beating his head against a wall' and give himself over to it.

Sexuality is key to the novel. Claude first catches sight of Perken in the arms of a vast, black prostitute, and this 'eroticism' is initially seen as Perken's Achilles heel. However, Claude soon comes to regard it as the source of his friend's strength: 'The brothels of Somalia are full of surprises.' Grabot is described by Perken, not without admiration, as an 'absolutely "pure" pervert'. He is a 'thinker', one for whom the erotic and philosophical spheres are intimately linked. Much of the dialogue is given over to such discussions of desire and power: for Malraux adventure seems only half the story, impulses and consequences are what truly fire his imagination.

I was most struck by the intensely visual quality of his writing. The description of Claude watching Perken walk out to their native captors is stunningly evocative. Claude's hands shaking as he holds the binoculars, the blurry, frenzied searching until at last he gets a visual fix. Having to watch this crucial scene unfold in frantic snatches is breathtaking: first the hesitant, limping Perken, then the surrounding wall of hostile tribesmen, each maddeningly isolated from the other as the binoculars cannot contain both at once. The drama of the encounter is intensified almost beyond endurance, but the precision of the description holds you utterly compelled.

The seething life of the rainforest is rendered in sensuous detail, the descriptions often uncomfortable but also lusciously tangible: 'the leaves he could feel through his clothes.' The jungle from a distance is a 'clenched fist'; once inside it, however, 'everything spread, grew soft, made an effort to adapt to this world'. The insects are given particular attention: 'the lingering sensation in his raised hand of a cluster of tiny eggs and creatures with shells, which he had crushed… his nerves were aware only of the crushed insects.' Malraux is also careful to maintain the sense of menace which the rainforest holds, unafraid of employing some viciously grotesque imagery: 'the sweat that ran down their faces, mingled with the sandstone dust, and formed long rivulets under the sunglasses, like blood streaming from gouged eyes.'

The Way of the Kings is a mass of contradictions. Two loners, misanthropes, who are drawn irresistibly to each other, forming an intensely loyal bond. A fierce critique of colonialism, which makes one of its central characters a charismatic demagogue, seeking to escape white society as leader of 'his' tribes in the rainforest. Malraux describes the bright scar left behind when Claude chisels away the bas-reliefs, and yet depicts the impulse to seek out these treasures as an essential, vital life force. Grabot is the extreme, the man whom both Claude and Perken could become if they surrender completely to their obsessive desires, and yet his enslavement by the Stiengs is ambivalent as there is always the sense that it was, at least initially, voluntary. He is seen as revolting, stripped of all dignity, all individuality, more beast than man when Claude and Perken find him. But even then they find something to admire there, what Perken calls 'a kind of greatness, one that's elementary and with a strong dose of hatred, but out of the ordinary all the same.'

Structurally the novel is also full of challenges to the reader. Until almost halfway through, the narrative perspective is entirely Claude's. Suddenly, abruptly, we are allowed into Perken's thoughts, and from there on the narrative jumps continually between the two. The story drives on, relentlessly compelling but never offering simple narrative satisfactions: one quest is simply supplanted by another and another, and the reader must keep pace with the protagonists or be abandoned amongst the rot and insects of the forest floor.

While reading, I often found myself reaching for pen and paper to note a startling turn of phrase: 'the fleeing Stiengs who filled the depths which concealed them, like an ultimate decay' being a particular favourite. I also admire his toughness: Malraux does not allow himself platitudes, or his readers' easy sympathies, as his characters' failings are always readily acknowledged, 'the disasters which the madness of white men always brought with them sooner or later'. And while the friendship between his protagonists has been pivotal to the narrative, Malraux ends the novel with the simple, devastating severing of the bond between Claude and his mentor: 'Perken was looking at this witness, as foreign to him now as a creature from another world.'

I did not always find this book easy. The extreme maleness of the sexuality was at times an irritation, and the likening of the native tribes to insects or disease makes for uncomfortable reading: 'the furtive, unseen presence of the Stiengs, like a miasma of decay, infested every cranny of the jungle.' But even if these things jar, the force of Malraux's prose is undeniable. The final section is an apocalyptic vision of animals fleeing from men who are fleeing from other men, the forest a teeming mass of fear and destruction as the railroad burns its way through to where the Way of the Kings once passed. For me, this novel is a passionate invocation to live every second. However, I take it simultaneously as a warning of the desperate consequences, both personal and global, of being so 'fiercely alive'.

– *Rachel Seiffert, 2005*

Introduction

On 13th October 1923, in Marseilles, André Malraux, not yet twenty-two years old and still a little-known figure in the French literary world, embarked with his wife Clara on the liner Angkor at the start of a three-week voyage that would take them to Saigon in what was then French Indochina. Malraux's declared intention was to explore temples in the Angkor Wat area of Cambodia, a 'mission' for which he had obtained official backing from the Minister for Colonies before leaving Paris. The results of his exploration were to be made available to the French School of the Far East, the government organisation in charge of archaeological expeditions within Indochina.

Secretly, his intentions were far less honourable. Malraux's wife Clara came from a well-to-do family of German-Jewish origin, and for the first years of their marriage he had relied on her money to support them while he struggled to make a name for himself as a critic. Unfortunately, he had also taken to speculating with the same money on the stock market, and when the Mexican mining company in which he had invested went bankrupt in the summer of 1923, the couple faced ruin. A way out of their financial difficulties had to be found urgently.

He had already developed an interest in oriental art. Reading an article about a small temple discovered in 1914 at Banteai Srei in the north-east of Angkor Wat, but subsequently barely explored, gave him an idea. At the same time as he applied to the Minister for Colonies for backing for an archaeological expedition to the temple, he also contacted an American art merchant, who agreed to purchase the carvings that Malraux intended to bring back with him.

Malraux and Clara arrived in Saigon on 4th November 1923. From there, they travelled to Hanoi to present themselves to the authorities. They were not well received. The authorities seem to have been suspicious of their motives from the start, and made it perfectly clear to them that it was absolutely forbidden to remove anything from the archaeological site. They also warned them that two previous chargés de mission had been killed in the same area.

In December, they travelled to Phnom Penh to buy equipment, then set off by boat, with an old friend of Malraux's, Louis Chevasson, along the Mekong river to the small town of Siam Reap not far from Banteay Srei. Once they reached Banteay Srei, it took Malraux and Chevasson two days to cut away several carvings of divinities from the temple: a haul weighing 800 kilos. They returned along the Mekong, arriving back in Phnom Penh on the night of 23rd–24th December. The police were waiting for them. Their luggage was searched and the stolen carvings discovered. The three of them were placed under house arrest pending their trial.

It was to be more than six months before the trial took place. This long period of enforced confinement brought Clara to the point of attempted suicide and seems to have hardened Malraux against the French authorities, opening his eyes to the iniquities and corruption of colonial rule. The trial was finally held in Saigon in July 1924. Malraux was sentenced to three years' imprisonment and Chevasson to eighteen months. The charges against Clara were dismissed, and she returned to France to organise a campaign for her husband's release. Her efforts bore fruit in a petition signed in September by a number of prominent French intellectuals, including André Gide, François Mauriac, Max Jacob, Louis Aragon and André Breton. In October, the case went to appeal. Malraux's sentence was reduced to one year, and Chevasson's to ten months, both sentences suspended. At the end of November, both men were released and returned to France.

Despite these tribulations, Malraux was later to describe this first experience of Asia as 'one of the deepest and most complex encounters of my youth'. It certainly seems to have unleashed something in him, from both a literary and a political point of view. At the beginning of 1925, he signed a contract with the publisher Bernard Grasset, under whose auspices his first books would appear in quick succession during the late 1920s. Soon after, he returned to Indochina, not with the purpose of plundering works of art this time, but of fighting French colonialism. In collaboration with Paul Monin, a young Saigon lawyer who had been involved in the campaign for his release, he launched *L'Indochine*, a virulently anti-colonialist newspaper which struggled on for 49 issues, despite constant attack by the authorities, before being finally closed down. Malraux decided to continue the paper clandestinely, and it was while he was searching for support for this venture that he made contact with agents of the Chinese Nationalist Party, the Kuomintang, then strongly under the influence of the Communists: an experience which would eventually lead to the writing of his most famous novel, *La Condition Humaine*, set in China, as well as to the myth, widely disseminated – not least by Malraux himself – that he himself had been actively involved in Chinese revolutionary politics.

La Voie royale ('The Way of the Kings') appeared in France in 1930, six years after the expedition to Banteai Srei and its unfortunate aftermath. The first half of the novel follows the true events quite closely, and can be taken as a belated justification of his actions at that time: Malraux's mercenary venture of 1923 is transformed into an existential adventure, the search of a sensitive and restless young man, Claude, for a meaning to his life. But once the ostensible object of Claude's expedition – the removal of ancient artefacts from a temple – has been achieved (about halfway through the book), the focus of the narrative shifts. The 'obsession' announced as early as the first sentence – that of Claude for his older travelling companion, the enigmatic Dane, Perken – gradually takes over, until Perken becomes the central character: the last part is told almost entirely from within the consciousness of the dying Perken. The Dane, himself obsessed, not so much by death as by the irrevocable effects of ageing, has let himself be persuaded to accompany Claude on his mission in order to carry out two missions of his own. The first is to track down a Frenchman named Grabot who has gone missing in the jungle: here it is impossible not to be reminded of Marlow's search for Kurtz in Conrad's *Heart of Darkness*, a work which Malraux is known to have admired. The second, which does not become clear until the last part of the novel, is to return to the territory he has previously claimed as his own and reclaim it in a final attempt to assert himself against age, death and the encroachment of civilisation. Malraux seems to have based the character of Perken on a number of European adventurers who did indeed try to establish themselves as rulers in remote areas of Indochina: two of them – Odend'hal and Mayrena – are even mentioned by name in the course of the book.

Curiously, given that the years between Malraux's expedition and the writing of *The Way of the Kings* saw the growth of his political awareness, it is hard to detect an anti-colonialist stance in the book. If the French authorities are shown in a bad light, as they are, it is mainly because they put bureaucratic obstacles in the protagonists' way. But the indigenous peoples do not come off any better: none of the 'native' characters is established as an individual, and the 'savage' tribesmen are depicted as bestial, even subhuman, on a level with the animals and insects of the jungle. Malraux seems to see no irony in presenting as his heroes a man (Claude) who travels to a foreign country to steal that country's artefacts for profit, and two men (Perken and Grabot) who attempt to establish personal supremacy over the people of that country. At least at this point in his career, the quest of the individual searching for personal fulfilment carries more weight than moral or political considerations. The three main characters represent different stages of this quest: Claude, the youthful idealist, Perken, the older adventurer aware of his own decline and determined to battle against it, and Grabot, the man who has overreached himself and in the process been stripped of his manhood and reduced to slavery. Of the three, it is Perken who seems best to represent Malraux's ideal of heroism: the man who, even at the point of death, refuses to surrender.

To depict these extreme situations, Malraux adopts an extreme style, as tangled and dense as the jungle through which his protagonists struggle. Ornate descriptions, torrents of adjectives, extravagant similes, sentences of Proustian complexity, bulging with subordinate clauses, interspersed with dialogue so laconic as to verge at times on the cryptic: these are not the calm, measured, analytical tones of classical French prose. This is an explosion, an outpouring of youthful energy (used, paradoxically, to hammer home images of decay, decomposition, inertia and death), which accords well with what we know of Malraux as a young man.

The thing that comes across most strongly in accounts of Malraux's early years is indeed his sheer energy. He was the archetypal young man in a hurry. In the ten years after the ill-fated expedition to Banteay Srei, Malraux not only returned to Indochina and edited a newspaper, as we have seen, but also travelled widely, visiting the U.S.S.R., Persia, China, India, Afghanistan, Japan and the United States, produced four books and a spate of articles, and engaged in various forms of political activism. When France's most prestigious literary prize, the Prix Goncourt, was awarded to his fourth novel, *La Condition Humaine*, in 1933, thus consolidating his reputation, he was just thirty-two. Still in the future were his exploits as a pilot during the Spanish Civil War and as a colonel in the French Resistance during World War II, and his long association with General de Gaulle, including a long stint as France's Minister of Culture. This was a man with a determination to impose his personality at all costs, a man who had little doubt about his own importance. (There has to be a strong sense of self-belief in someone who could call a novel *The Human Condition*, surely one of the most grandiose titles ever for a work of fiction.) The sheer forcefulness of his character struck many of his contemporaries, even in those early years. One of the most perceptive, the writer and critic Maurice Sachs, penned this memorable description of him:

'There is in his gaze an air of adventure, melancholy and irresistible decisiveness... He speaks very fast and very well, appears to know everything, and really dazzles you, leaving you with the impression that you have met the most intelligent man of the century.'

It might be thought that his later career as a politician would have tempered his energy and introduced a certain gravitas. But thirty years after Sachs's encounter with Malraux, the American playwright Arthur Miller, attending a White House dinner during the Kennedy presidency in honour of the then French Minister of Culture, was struck by what he calls his 'unrelenting intensity':

'Malraux spoke in passionate bursts of French at a speed that defied comprehension... He smoked almost violently and had a fascinating and disconcerting tic that made you wonder how he ever relaxed enough to sleep.'

It is hard not to see the highly strung character described by these eyewitnesses reflected in the tortured, feverish prose of *The Way of the Kings*, a work that seems to have been wrung out of its author with an obsessive force to rival that which impels his doomed heroes.

Malraux remains a controversial figure in France. Was his stance as a man of letters doubled with a man of action just a pose? Did his evolution from youthful anti-colonialist firebrand and Communist fellow traveller to Establishment figurehead betray a lack of belief in anything other than self-promotion? Recent biographers have cast doubt on some of the myths surrounding him. Best perhaps to forget Malraux the public figure and reconsider Malraux the writer, of whose work *The Way of the Kings* remains a striking example. The book may have more than its share of woolly philosophising about life and death, and the modern reader may be made uncomfortable by its macho posturing, its glorification of the heroic white adventurer in his fight against the 'subhuman' natives. But looking beyond that, it is impossible not to be impressed by Malraux's extraordinary evocation of an alien, inhospitable landscape, a world of heat, sweat, danger and pain depicted with all the 'unrelenting intensity' that was so much part of the author's own personality.

– Howard Curtis, 2005

The Way of the Kings

Part One

I

This time, Claude's obsession entered into conflict: he stared hard at the man's face, trying to distinguish some expression in the shadows into which it was cast by the lighted bulb behind him. A shape as indistinct as the lights of the Somali coast swallowed by the intensity of the moonlight that shimmered on the salt marshes... An insistently ironic tone of voice which seemed equally to be swallowed by the African darkness, to be part of the legend that made this shadowy figure the centre of attention for passengers eager for gossip and Manila cigars, the web of talk, romance and daydream woven around any white man who had been involved in the independent states of Asia.

'Young men don't really understand – what shall we call it? – eroticism. Until you turn forty, you get it all wrong, you're trapped by love: any man who thinks, not of a woman as complementing sex, but of sex as complementing a woman, is ripe for love: too bad for him. But what's worse, there comes a time when the idea of sex, the idea of youth, comes back to haunt you, stronger than ever. Nourished by all kinds of memories...'

Aware of the smell of dust, hemp and wool on his own clothes, Claude saw again the curtain of sacking being partly lifted a little earlier, the hand behind it pointing to a young black woman, naked (shaved of her body hair), a dazzling patch of sunlight on her pointed right breast, the crease in her thick eyelids, so expressive of eroticism, the fanatical need, 'the need to reach your own breaking point' as Perken put it...

'And those memories are transformed...' he continued. 'Imagination! What an extraordinary thing it is! It doesn't even recognise itself... Imagination... It always compensates...'

His craggy face was barely visible in the darkness, but there was a gleam of light between his lips, coming from the end of his cigarette, gold-tipped for sure. Claude had the feeling that his thoughts were gradually moving closer to his words, like the small craft that was slowly approaching, the parallel arms of the rowers reflecting the lights of the ship. 'What do you mean exactly?'

'You'll understand, one of these days... The brothels of Somalia are full of surprises.'

Claude was familiar with the kind of hate-filled irony a man only uses about himself and his own destiny.

'Full of surprises,' Perken repeated.

'What kind of surprises?' Claude wondered. He remembered the oil lamps, patches of light surrounded by insects, the girls with their straight noses, and nothing about them that corresponded to the word 'negress' except the brilliant whites of their eyes between the pupils and the black skin. To the rhythm of a flute played by a blind man, they moved forward in a circle, each one angrily striking the ample rump of the one in front of her. And all at once, the melody stopped, the line broke, and each girl came to a standstill, head and shoulders motionless, eyes closed, body tensed, her voice sustaining the carnal notes of the flute, then relaxed the tension by shaking the hard muscles of her buttocks and her upright breasts, on and on, the shaking accentuated by the sweat glistening in the light of the oil lamps... The madam had pushed in Perken's direction a very young girl, who was smiling.

'No,' he had said, 'the other one, over there. At least that one doesn't seem to be enjoying it.'

'Is he a sadist?' Claude was wondering now. There was talk of the missions the Siamese had entrusted to him among the rebel tribes, the way he had organised the Shan country and the Laotian marches, his curious relations – sometimes cordial, sometimes hostile – with the government in Bangkok, the passion he was said to have possessed once, a passion for domination, for that savage power he would not let anyone control, his decline, his sexual activities. On this ship, though, he could have been surrounded by women, but he'd refrained. 'There's something, but it isn't sadism…'

Perken rested his head against the back of his deckchair, and his mask-like face, the face of some brutish consular official, came fully into the light, accentuated by the shadows around the eyes and nose. Smoke rose vertically from his cigarette and vanished in the profound blackness of the night.

The word 'sadism' was still in Claude's mind, and it brought back a memory. 'In Paris one day, I was taken to a seedy little brothel. In the lounge, there was only one woman, tied to a rack with ropes, all a bit Grand Guignol, her skirts lifted…'

'Which way was she facing?'

'She had her back to us. There were six or seven men standing around her: lower-middle-class fellows in ready-made ties and alpaca jackets – it was summer, but not as hot as here – their eyes popping out of their heads, their cheeks crimson, trying hard to make it look as if they were there to amuse themselves… One after the other, they approached the woman and gave her a slap on the bottom – just one slap each – paid and left, or went upstairs…'

'Was that all?'

'Yes. And not many went upstairs: most of them left. The dreams of these characters as they put on their straw boaters, lifted the collars of their jackets and left…'

'Simple souls, though…' Perken raised his right arm as if to underline what he was saying, but then hesitated, struggling with his thoughts. 'The main thing is not to know your partner. All she needs to be is the opposite sex.'

'Not a person with her own individual life?'

'Especially among masochists. They're only ever fighting themselves… To fuel your imagination, you use what you can, not what you want. Even the stupidest prostitutes know how distant the man who's torturing them, or they are torturing, is from them. Do you know what they call the ones with unusual tastes? Cerebrals…'

'Unusual tastes,' thought Claude. 'He, too…' He couldn't take his eyes off Perken's taut face. Was this conversation leading somewhere?

'Cerebrals,' Perken repeated. 'And they're right. There's only one "sexual perversion", as idiots call it: the development of the imagination, the inability to be satisfied. Over in Bangkok, I knew a man who had himself tied up naked by a woman, in a dark room, for an hour…'

'And then?'

'That was it. That was all he wanted. He was an absolutely "pure" pervert.'

He stood up. 'Does he want to sleep,' Claude wondered, 'or to break off this conversation…?' Through the rising smoke, Perken was moving away, stepping one by one over the piccaninnies who were sleeping among the baskets of corals, their pink mouths open. His shadow grew shorter; while Claude's long shadow remained alone on deck. On it, his advancing chin seemed almost as sturdy as Perken's jaws. The light bulb moved, and the shadow began to tremble: in two months, what would be left of this shadow, and the body it continued? A shape without eyes, without that resolute but anxious gaze that expressed what he was much more, tonight, than that manly silhouette about to be crossed by the ship's cat. He put out his hand, and the cat ran away. The obsession descended on him again.

Another fortnight of this hunger; another fortnight waiting on this ship, as nervous as an addict deprived of his drug. Once again he took out the archaeological map of Siam and Cambodia; he knew it better than his own face… He was fascinated by the big blue circles he had drawn around the Dead Cities, the dotted line representing the old Way of the Kings, the threat it contained: being abandoned in the middle of the Siamese jungle. 'At least a fifty-fifty chance of snuffing it there…' A tangle of paths, the carcasses of small animals abandoned near dying fires, the end of the last mission to Jarai country: the white chief, Odend'hal, pummelled to death with spears, at night, by the men of the Sadete, the King of Fire, amid the rustle of crushed palms, announcing the arrival of the mission's elephants… How many nights would he have to stay awake, exhausted, plagued by mosquitoes, or go to sleep trusting to the vigilance of some guide?… You didn't often get a chance to fight… Perken knew the country, but wouldn't talk about it. Claude had been won over first by the tone of his voice: he was the only person on the ship who uttered the word 'energy' in such a simple way. It suggested to him that this man, even though his hair was almost grey, liked many of the same things he liked. The first time he had heard him, he was standing in front of a big red chunk of the coast of Egypt, telling the story, to a crowd of half-interested, half-hostile passengers, of two skeletons – tomb raiders, almost certainly – which had been discovered, during the latest dig in the Valley of the Kings, on the floor of an underground room surrounded by galleries carpeted as far as the eye could see with the mummies of sacred cats. Limited as his experience was, he had seen enough to know that there were as many fools among adventurers as among other men, but this man intrigued him. Since then, he had heard him talk about Mayrena, who had briefly been king of the Sedangs.

'I think he was a man keen to play out his own life story, like an actor playing a role. You French like men who attach more importance to… what shall we say?… yes, to playing their role well than to winning.'

Claude remembered his father, who had fought with great courage as a volunteer, and who had been killed on the Marne a few hours after writing these words: 'Now, my dear friend, we are mobilising the law, civilisation, and the severed hands of children. I've witnessed a few outbreaks of idiocy in my time: the Dreyfus affair wasn't bad, but this is definitely superior in every respect to any previous attempt, even in quality.'

'It's an attitude,' Perken continued, 'which glorifies the bravura that's part of the role... Mayrena was very brave... He set off through the untamed jungle with the body of his little Cham concubine on the back of an elephant, so that she could be buried like the princesses of her race, after the missionaries had refused to bury her in their cemetery... You know he became king by fighting two Sedang chiefs with a sabre, and spent some time in Jarai country... which is no easy task...'

'Do you know anyone who's lived among the Jarais?'

'Yes, me: for eight hours.'

'That's not long,' Claude replied, smiling.

Perken took his left hand from his pocket and held it up in front of Claude, the fingers outstretched: each of the three biggest had a deep spiral furrow in it, like a corkscrew. 'With lashes, it's long enough.'

Wounded by his own tactlessness, Claude hesitated.

'In the end,' Perken said, returning to the subject of Mayrena, 'he met a bad death, like almost all men...'

Claude had heard about that death, in a straw hut in Malaysia: the man brought low by his own failed hopes as if by a tumour, terrified at the sound of his own voice echoing in the giant trees. 'Not as bad as all that.'

'Suicide doesn't interest me.'

'Why's that?'

'A man who kills himself is chasing an image he's formed of

himself: the only reason to kill yourself is to exist. I don't like people to be duped by God.'

Every day the resemblance Claude had sensed had become more evident, accentuated by the inflections of Perken's voice, by the way he said 'they' when talking about the passengers – perhaps all men – as though he were separate from them, through his indifference to being defined socially. Beneath that tone of voice, Claude sensed that this was a man with a vast – if in some respects damaged – experience of humanity, which perfectly matched the expression in his eyes: heavy, enveloping, but remarkably steady whenever he made an assertion and the muscles of his face tensed for a moment.

Now, he was almost alone on deck. He would not sleep. Should he daydream or should he read? Leaf for the hundredth time through *Inventaire*, and again – as if beating his head against a wall – throw his imagination against those capitals of dust and lianas and towers with heads on them, hidden beneath the blue dots of the dead cities, and, despite the stubborn faith that drove him, again meet the very same obstacles that always, at the same point and with insistent regularity, tore his daydreams apart?

Bal-el-Mandeb: the Gates of Death.

Every time he talked to Perken, Claude was irritated by his allusions to a past he himself knew nothing about. The familiarity that had grown out of their encounter in Djibouti – he had only entered that house, rather than another, because he had glimpsed Perken's indistinct form beneath the outstretched arm of a big negress draped in red and black – could not free him of the anxious curiosity that drew him to the man as if he had a premonition of his own destiny, drew him to the struggle of a man who did not want to live in the community of men, now that age was creeping up on him and he was alone. The old Armenian with whom he occasionally went for a walk had known him for a long time but said little about him, a strategy that seemed to spring from fear: for, although he was an acquaintance of Perken's, he certainly wasn't his friend. And, like the constant noise of the engines beneath the changing noise of words, the obsession with the jungle and the temples returned, covering everything, reasserting its nerve-wracking domination over Claude. As if Asia itself had found a powerful ally in Perken, the obsession aroused more daydreams in Claude in his half-sleeping, half-waking state, daydreams derived from the Chronicles: armies setting off in the odorous, cicada-filled evening, lazy swarms of mosquitoes above the dust raised by the horses, cries as the caravans forded tepid rivers, missions brought to a halt when the waters fell before shoals of fish that looked blue beneath a sky riddled with butterflies, old kings broken down by their wives – and the other, indestructible daydream: the temples, the stone gods made green by moss, frogs on their shoulders, their eroded heads on the ground beside them…

Now the legend of Perken was roaming the ship, passing from deckchair to deckchair like the anguish or expectation of arrival, like the malevolent boredom of a long sea passage. It was still an undefined legend, full of mindless mystery rather than hard fact. There were plenty of people eager to confide, knowingly, behind cupped hands, 'An amazing fellow, you know, amazing', but few who knew what they were talking about. He had lived among the natives, in territory where many of his predecessors had been killed, and had held sway over them, probably using methods that had not been very legal to begin with. That was all anyone could say for sure. And his effectiveness, Claude thought, probably owed more to his persistent energy, his endurance, his military qualities, combined with a mind broad enough to make an effort to understand people different from himself, than to such adventures. Claude had never before realised the extent to which functionaries needed romanticism to nourish their dreams, even though it was a need immediately thwarted by the fear of being duped, of admitting the existence of a world different from theirs. These people accepted the whole of the legend of Mayrena – who was dead – and perhaps the legend of Perken, too, at least when he was far away. Here, they defended themselves against his silence, suspicious, eager to avenge themselves by showing contempt for what was sometimes a very explicit desire for solitude. Claude had at first wondered why Perken had accepted his presence: he was the only one who admired him, and perhaps understood him, without trying to judge him. He was trying to understand him better, but found it hard to reconcile the romantic anecdotes – when he was organising the Shan country, he was said to have sent messages out through the rebel tribes encircling him, in tubes placed inside corpses that floated downriver, there were even stories of wizardry – with what he felt was the essence of this man who had no interest in playing out his own life story, who felt no need to admire his own actions, and who was impelled by a strong will which Claude often sensed but was unable fully to grasp.

The captain sensed it, too. 'Every adventurer starts out as a mythomaniac,' he would say to Claude: but it was Perken's decisiveness, his sense of organisation, his refusal to speak about his own life that he found particularly surprising. 'He makes me think of those people high up in the English Intelligence Service, employed and disowned at the same time. But he won't end up the head of a counter-espionage bureau in London: he has something extra, he's German…'

'German or Danish?'

'Danish since the Germans were forced by the treaty of Versailles to withdraw from Schleswig. Good for him: the heads of the Siamese police and army are Danish. Oh, *heimatlos*, of course!… No, I don't think he'll end up in an office: just look, he's on his way back to Asia…'

'In the service of the Siamese government?'

'Yes and no, as always… He's supposed to be looking for some fellow who stayed on in rebel country – stayed on or vanished, something like that – but the surprising thing is that he's started to be interested in money… That's new…'

A singular bond had been formed. Claude thought about it, as soon as the obsession faded temporarily and he was idle again: Perken belonged to the only race of men with whom his grandfather – who had raised him – had felt a link. There was a distant kinship there: the same hostility towards established values, the same liking for the actions of men combined with an awareness of their futility, and above all, the same rejection. The images that Claude glimpsed of his future were divided between his memories and that presence: they called to him like a two-fold threat, like two parallel assertions of the same prophecy. In his conversations with Perken, he could only match his inter-locutor's experience and memories with what he had gleaned from his reasonably wide reading, and so, to avoid endlessly countering actions with books, he had ended up talking about his grandfather the way Perken talked about his own life. In doing this, Claude benefited from the singular interest Perken showed in Claude's grandfather, and besides, whenever Perken talked about himself he conjured up for Claude his grand-father's white Napoleon III beard, his disgust with the world, the bitter stories of his youth. His grandfather, proud both of his corsair ancestors from some lost mythical past and his own stevedore grandfather, proud of kicking the deck on his ships like a peasant stroking his animals, had devoted his youth to building up the Vannec Company, which he intended to be his legacy. He had married at the age of thirty-five: twelve days after the wedding, his wife had gone back to her parents. Her father did not want to see her. Her mother had concluded, in weary desperation, 'You know, my dear, all these things… as long as you have children…' And so she had come back to the old mansion he had bought for her, with its carriage entrance surmounted by maritime symbols and its vast courtyard where sails were left to dry. She had taken down the portraits of her parents, thrown them under the bed, and replaced them with a little crucifix. Her husband had said nothing: for several days, neither of them spoke. Then their married life resumed. They were both heirs to a tradition of work, and hated any kind of romanticism, so the resentment this first misunderstanding had aroused in them did not find expression in conflict. They made allowances in their lives for a tacit hostility, just as, if they had been disabled, they would have made allowances for their disabilities. They were both unskilled at expressing their feelings, and so each tried to outdo the other in devotion to work: both found in it a refuge and a secret passion. The birth of their children established a new connection between them that merely made their old hostility all the more painful. Each statement of accounts concealed increased hatred: when night came to the big house and the brown sails in the courtyard, when the sailors, the ship's boys and the workers had left or were in bed asleep, and some late hour sounded, it was not unusual for one of the two, leaning out of the window, to see light in the other's window and, although exhausted, to get down to some new work. She was consumptive, but neglected herself, and every year he worked more, so that his lamp was never extinguished before his wife's, which itself remained lit until late in the night.

One day, he noticed that the crucifix had joined her parents' portraits under the bed.

Disconcerted at the pain caused, not only by the deaths of those he loved, but also by that of a wife he did not love, he bore her death, when it came, with a mixture of distaste and resignation. He had respected his wife: he knew she had been unhappy. Such was life. It was his distaste, even more than her death, which brought about the decline of the house. After almost his entire fleet ran aground off the coast of Newfoundland, the insurance companies refused to pay. After spending a whole day distributing among the widows piles of notes as numerous as his dead sailors, with a stronger sense of distaste for money than he had ever felt before, he said farewell to his business – and the tribulations began.

Tribulations without number and without end. Gripped by a hostility towards respectable virtues that had been hatching for a long time, the old man welcomed into the sail-filled courtyard circuses which had been refused hospitality by the town council, and the old maidservant threw open the carriage entrance through which no carriage had passed in years, for the elephant to enter. Alone in the vast dining room, sitting in his cabled armchair, sipping a glass of his best wine, he summoned his memories, one by one, as he turned the pages of his account books…

When they were twenty, the children left the increasingly silent house, and it remained silent until the war brought Claude there. After his father was killed, his mother, who had left her husband long before, came to visit the boy. Again, she was living alone. Old Vannec welcomed her: he had become so accustomed to despising the actions of men that he regarded them all with the same mixture of hatred and indulgence. In the evening, he stopped her from leaving, indignant at the idea that, with him alive, his daughter-in-law could be staying in a hotel, in his town: he knew from experience that hospitality and resentment could coexist. They talked, or rather, she talked: a deserted wife, tortured by the thought of ageing but certain of her own decline, her attitude to life was one of desperate indifference. Someone with whom he could live… She was ruined, if not poor. He did not really like her, but he had a curious kind of fellow feeling for her: she, like him, was separated from the community of men who expected agreement on so much that was stupid or underhand. The cousin was old now, and no longer very good at housekeeping… He suggested that she stay, and she had accepted.

She made up her face for solitude, the portraits of the old owners and the maritime symbols, and above all for the mirrors against which she could only defend herself with drawn curtains and the artifices of half-light, but age got to her sooner than expected and killed her, as if her anguish had been a premonition. He accepted this death with grim approval: 'You don't change your beliefs at my age…' That fate should thus complete the tissue of stupidity from which she had made her life was fine with him. From that point on, he rarely abandoned the hostile silence in which he confined himself, except to deal with Claude. Driven by a subtle selfishness typical of the old, he had usually left the task of punishing the boy to the old cousin, the boy's mother or his teachers, so that in Dunkirk – and even later, when, studying in Paris, the adolescent met his uncles – he always seemed to Claude unusually free in his ideas. In this simple old man, given grandeur by the dead that surrounded him and by the tragic light which the sea lent to those who had devoted themselves to her, there was a preacher, uneducated but not God-fearing: some of the words he used to convey the weight of his experience echoed within Claude like the muffled creaking of the back door of that big house, solitary now in the deserted street and at night completely cut off from the world. When, after dinner, his grandfather spoke, the end of his beard touching his chest, his long-meditated words troubled Claude, who defended himself against them: they were words that had crossed time or the sea, from lands inhabited by men who were more familiar than any others with the weight, the bitterness and the obscure force of life. 'A memory, my boy, is like a bloody family vault! To have more of the dead around you than the living… I know our dead well: in all of them – in you, too – there is the same nature. Even when they deny it… Did you know there are crabs who, without realising it, suckle the parasites who are eating away at them?… To be a Vannec means something, for better or worse…'

When Claude had left to continue his studies in Paris, the old man had got into the habit of going every day to the wall commemorating sailors lost at sea: he envied them their deaths, and found a certain joy in relating his old age to that nothingness. One day, attempting to show a young worker who was too slow how, in his time, they used to cut wood to make prows, he had felt suddenly dizzy as he held the double-bladed axe, and had cut open his own skull. And now Claude found in Perken the same tastes, the same hostility, the same passionate connection he had had with that old man of seventy-six who had been determined not to forget his former mastery and who had died the death of an old Viking in that deserted house. How would this one finish? He had replied to him one day, looking out over the Ocean, 'I think your grandfather was less significant than you think, but that you yourself are much more so.' It was as if they had both been expressing themselves in parables: beneath the concealment of memory, they were moving closer to each other.

When the fog lifted, the ship was enveloped in rain. The long triangular beam of the Colombo lighthouse rotated in the darkness, above a line of lights: the docks. The passengers gathered on deck stood looking out beyond the rain-drenched rail at all those flickering lights. Near Claude, a fat man was helping the Armenian – a dealer in stones who had come to Ceylon to buy sapphires which he would sell in Shanghai – to arrange his suitcases.

Some distance away, Perken was chatting to the captain; seen like that, a quarter turned away, his face seemed less masculine, especially when he smiled.

'You see the Chang's face,' the fat man said. 'Like that, he looks like a good person…'

'What do you call him?'

'It's the Siamese who call him that. It means "the elephant", not the tame elephant, the other kind. Physically, it doesn't really suit him, but morally, it suits him quite well…'

The beam from the lighthouse lashed them, bathing them for a moment in dazzling light, before plunging back into the darkness. Sparkling drops of rain swirled in the ship's lights, but the only thing visible now was a high-sided Arab sailing ship, carved from prow to poop, motionless and deserted, isolated amid the masses of shadow. Perken had just taken two steps forward. Instinctively, the fat man lowered his voice. Claude smiled.

'Oh, of course he doesn't scare me! I've been in the colonies for twenty-seven years. Just think of it! But he… he intimidates me, if I can put it that way. What about you?'

'It's a fine thing to be able to do that regardless,' the Armenian replied – not very loudly – 'but it doesn't always work…'

'You speak very good French…'

It was clear he was avenging himself for some humiliation. Had he waited until he was about to leave the boat to do so? His voice was not ironic, but full of rancour.

Perken was moving away again.

'I'm from Constantinople… and Montmartre on my holidays. No, monsieur, it doesn't always work…' He turned to Claude. 'You'll soon get tired of him, like the others… When you think of what he's done!… But if he'd had any technical expertise, yes, technical, monsieur, in the position he was in, holding the country for the Siamese, he could have made a fortune which… well, anyway, a fortune…'

He waved both his arms in a circle, hiding for a moment the lights of land, more numerous and closer now, but less distinct, as if they, too, had become damp and porous.

'Just think, in the markets of Siam, twelve, fifteen days from the rebel villages, if you're clever, and if you know how to do business with them, you can still find rubies at prices you wouldn't believe! You have no idea, because that isn't your field… And it's a damned sight better than going up there to barter polished pieces of jewellery, made out of paste, for large, crude pieces, even if they are made of gold!… Even at the age of twenty-three!… The business wasn't even his, mind you: a white man started it with the King of Siam about fifty years ago… But he wanted to go there, come what may – surprising they didn't do him in straight away! He always wanted to play the chief. As I said, there are times when it doesn't work. They really made him see that in Europe. Two hundred thousand francs! To find two hundred thousand francs like that, it's not so easy to play the lord! All the same, you can't deny he impresses the natives…'

'So he needs money?'

'Not to live on, of course, especially up there…'

The launches were drawing alongside, full of Indians wringing their soaking turbans as they climbed out, and fruit. The Armenian followed a messenger from one of the hotels.

'He needs money,' Claude was repeating to himself.

'The old ape is right about that,' the fat man resumed. 'Life doesn't cost a lot up there!'

'Are you a forester?'

'Station chief.'

The obsession overwhelmed him once again, like an attack of fever: here was a man he could question about the fearsome game to which he was about to bind his life.

'Have you ever travelled with carts?'

'Of course I've travelled with carts, what do you think?'

'How much can they really carry?'

'They're small, aren't they? If you need to carry anything heavy…'

'Stones, for example…'

'Well, according to the regulations, the maximum weight is sixty kilos.'

If the weight was not simply something imposed by one of those colonial laws that only exist in the minds of the administrators, he'd have to abandon the idea of carts. So being abandoned in an unknown jungle pursued him even here. Could he get men to carry blocks weighing two hundred kilos on their backs for a month? Impossible. What about elephants?

'Elephants? I'll tell you this, young man. You just have to be clever. People think elephants are fussy. It isn't true: elephants aren't fussy. The problem is, that they don't like shafts or straps, they find them ticklish. So what do you do? Eh?'

'You tell me.'

The fat man good-naturedly placed his hand on Claude's shoulder. 'You take a car tyre, an ordinary Michelin tyre, and put it round the elephant's neck, like a napkin ring. Right? Then you attach your vehicles to the tyre… It's as simple as that. Rubber's soft, you know…'

'Can you get elephants in the far north of Angkor?'

'The far north?'

'Yes.'

A moment's silence. 'As far as the Dang Rek mountains?'

'As far as the Se Mun river.'

'Any white man attempting that on his own is doomed.'

'Can you get hold of elephants?'

'Well, that's up to you… But I'd be surprised if you could get elephants. For a start, the natives won't be too keen to go walkabout in that region; you're very likely to fall among the rebel Mois, and that's no joke. Secondly, the natives in the last villages are so riddled with malaria it's made them retarded and incapable of doing anything. Their eyelids are so blue, it's as if someone had been hitting them for a week. Then, if you get bitten, which usually happens, you can always say it wasn't by the right mosquitoes, damn them!... In addition... Well, that's enough to be getting on with... Shall we go for a ride? There's the launch...'

'No.' He was pursuing his thoughts. 'He needs money, but it can't be to live, especially up there...' That much was clear. So what did he need it for? Far more than the menace of the jungle, this malevolent legend, which was not without its greatness, was breaking down, like a fermenting agent, like the night itself, what Claude had thought of as reality. Each time the siren of one of the lighted boats called to the dinghies, the sound lingering for a long time in the saturated air of the harbour, more of the town disappeared, finally melting altogether into the Indian night. His last Western thoughts were drowning in this strange, transitory atmosphere. The wind, gentle now, cooled his eyelids and gave Perken the air not so much of someone unusual, but rather of someone who had adapted. Like all those who rebel against the world, Claude was instinctively searching for fellow spirits, and wanted them to be great. In this particular case, he had no fear that he was deceiving himself. If the man wanted money, it wasn't to collect tulips. Beneath the stories he had told, money was there, like the muted screeching of the cicadas beneath the silence at that moment... The captain, too, had said, 'He's interested in money now...'

And the station chief: 'Any white man who tries to go there alone is done for...'

Any white man who tries to go there alone is done for...

At this hour, Perken was probably in the bar.

2

Claude did not have to look for him: he was sitting, with his back turned, at one of the rattan tables which the waiters had arranged on deck, one hand holding a glass that stood on the tablecloth, the other hand resting on the rail, and seemed to be looking at the lights which still shimmered in the wind at the far end of the harbour.

Claude felt awkward.

'My last port of call!' Perken said, pointing to the lights with his free hand.

It was his left hand: lit on just one side by the ship, it appeared for a moment in strong outline against a sky now washed clean and filled with stars, the furrows on the fingers changed into black circles. He turned fully to Claude, who was surprised by the despondent expression on his face. The hand disappeared.

'We're leaving in an hour... Tell me, what does arriving mean to you?'

'Doing something instead of dreaming. And to you?'

Perken made a gesture, as if dismissing the question. He nevertheless replied, 'Wasting time...'

Claude looked at him questioningly: he closed his eyes. 'Things aren't looking good,' Claude thought. 'Let's try it another way.'

'Are you going back up to rebel country?'

'That isn't what I call wasting my time: on the contrary.'

Claude was still searching for a way in. 'On the contrary?' he repeated, almost casually.

'Up there, I've found almost everything.'

'Except money, I suppose?'

Perken looked at him attentively, without replying.

'And what if there were money, up there?'

'Go and find it then!'

'Perhaps...' Claude hesitated: in the distance, solemn chanting rose from a temple, interrupted by the horn of some lost car. 'In the jungle – from Laos to the sea – there are quite a lot of temples unknown to Europeans...'

'Oh, yes! The gods of gold! Please spare me!'

'I'm not talking about gold, I'm talking about bas-reliefs and statues which are worth a considerable amount...' He hesitated again. 'You want to find two hundred thousand francs, don't you?'

'Was it the Armenian who told you that? It's no secret, anyway. There are the tombs of the Pharaohs, too, why not them?'

'Do you think, Monsieur Perken, I'm going to go looking for the tombs of the Pharaohs with all those cats around?'

Perken seemed to be thinking. Claude looked at him, realising that public records, facts, were as powerless against the power of certain men as against the charm of a woman. At that moment, the business with the jewels, this man's life story, did not exist. He was so real, standing there, that the actions of his past life seemed separate from him, like dreams. Of the facts, Claude would only retain those which were in harmony with his own feelings... But when was he going to answer?

'Shall we go for a walk?'

They took a few steps in silence. Perken was still looking at the yellow lights of the port, motionless beneath the brighter stars. In spite of the night, the air stuck to Claude's skin like a clammy hand as soon as he fell silent. He took a cigarette from a packet, but was immediately annoyed by the nonchalance of his own gesture, and threw it in the sea.

'I came across a few temples,' Perken said at last. 'First of all, they're not all decorated.'

'No. But many are.'

'Cassirer in Berlin paid five thousand gold marks for the two Buddhas Damrong gave me. But to go looking for monuments! You might as well search for treasure like the natives…'

'If you were certain that fifty treasures were buried alongside a river, between two specific points six hundred metres apart, for example… would you look for them then?'

'There's no river.'

'There is. Do you want to search for the treasures?'

'For you?'

'With me, equal shares.'

'Where's the river?'

Claude found Perken's half smile extremely annoying. 'Come and see.'

In the corridor leading to Claude's cabin, Perken put his hand on the young man's shoulder. 'You insinuated yesterday that you were staking everything on one last game. Were you referring to what you've just told me?'

'Yes.'

Claude thought he would find the map stretched out on his bunk, but the boy had folded it. He opened it. 'Here are the lakes. All these little red marks in a cluster around them: the temples. These scattered marks: other temples.'

'And these blue marks?'

'The dead cities of Cambodia. Already explored. In my opinion there are others, but never mind. To continue: as you can see, there are a lot of red marks, indicating temples, where my black line begins, and they continue along it.'

'And what is that line?'

'The Way of the Kings, the road that used to link Angkor and the lakes to the Menam basin. As important once as the road from the Rhône to the Rhine in the Middle Ages.'

'The temples follow this line as far as –'

'The place doesn't matter: as far as the limit of the regions that have really been explored. I say all you have to do is take a compass and follow the route of the old Way to find the temples. If Europe was covered in jungle, it would be absurd to think that you could go from Marseilles to Cologne via the Rhône and the Rhine without finding the ruins of churches… And don't forget, in the explored region, this theory of mine can be verified… and has been. It's in all the old travellers' stories…' He broke off to respond to the look Perken was giving him. 'I haven't just dropped from the skies, you know. I studied oriental languages. Sanskrit has its uses… The administrators who've ventured a few dozen kilometres away from the mapped region have confirmed it.'

'You think you're the first to interpret the map this way?'

'The geographical service doesn't really take an interest in archaeology.'

'What about the French Institute?'

Claude opened *Inventaire* at a marked page: various sentences were underlined: *It remains to note the monuments which were outside our itineraries… We make no claims for the completeness of our lists…* 'That's the report of the last great archaeological mission.'

Perken looked at the date. '1908?'

'There was nothing big between 1908 and the war. Since then, there's been some isolated exploration, but it's all in the early stages. I've cross-checked, and I'm sure the way the units of measurement used by the old travellers have been interpreted needs to be rectified. As we went along the Way, we'd have to check a number of statements which have been taken as legends, but which seem promising… And we're only talking about Cambodia: in Siam, you know, nothing has been done at all.' If only he would reply, instead of this silence! 'What are you thinking?'

'The compass may give a general indication, but then you're relying on the natives to point you in the right direction?'

'Those whose villages are close to the ancient Way, yes.'

'Perhaps… Especially in Siam. I know Siamese well enough to get them to talk. I've seen some of these temples myself… They're old Brahman temples, aren't they?'

'Yes.'

'So, no fanaticism, we'd still be among Buddhists… The plan may not be so fanciful after all… Do you know a lot about that kind of art?'

'That's all I've been studying lately.'

'Lately… How old are you?'

'Twenty-six.'

'Ah…'

'I know, I look younger.'

'It wasn't so much surprise, it was… envy.' The tone was not ironic. 'The French administration don't much like –'

'I'm on an official mission.'

Surprise prevented Perken from replying immediately. 'I'm starting to understand…'

'Oh, unpaid, of course! Our ministries are quite happy with that.'

Claude saw again the polite, pompous head clerk, the deserted corridors, shafts of sunlight across artless maps on which towns – Vientiane, Timbuktu, Djibouti – reigned in the middle of great pink circles like capitals, the stage furniture, dark red and gold…

'Relations with the Institute in Hanoi, requisition vouchers, I see,' Perken went on. 'Not much, but all the same…' He looked at the map again. 'Transport: carts.'

'Oh, by the way! Tell me: what about the sixty-kilo rule?'

'Forget it. It doesn't matter. From fifty to three hundred kilos depending on… depending on what you find. Carts, then. And if we haven't found anything after a month…'

'Unlikely. You know perfectly well that the Dang Reks haven't been explored…'

'More than you think.'

'…and that the natives know the temples. What do you mean, more than I think?'

'We'll get back to that…' He was silent for a moment. 'I know the French administration. You're not part of it. They'll put obstacles in our way, but that's not such a great danger… The other danger, though, even with two of us…'

'The other danger?'

'Staying there.'

'The Mois?'

'The Mois, the jungle, the fever.'

'That's what I thought.'

'So, let's not talk any more about it: I'm used to it. Let's talk about money.'

'It's quite simple: a little bas-relief, a quite ordinary statue, is worth thirty thousand francs.'

'Gold francs?'

'Now you're being greedy.'

'Too bad. I need at least ten. Ten for you: that's twenty.'

'Twenty stones.'

'Obviously, that's not bad…'

'And besides, a single bas-relief, if it's a good one, a dancing girl for instance, is worth at least two hundred thousand francs.'

'How many stones does something like that consist of?'

'Three or four…'

'And you're sure you can sell them?'

'I'm certain. I know the biggest specialists in London and Paris. And it's easy to organise an auction.'

'Easy, perhaps, but doesn't it take a long time?'

'There's nothing to stop you selling directly – I mean, without an auction. These objects are extremely rare: the great increase in the number of Asian objects dates from the end of the war, and nothing has been discovered since.'

'Another thing: supposing we find the temples…'

('We,' Claude murmured.)

'…how do you free the carved stones?'

'That'll be the hardest part. I was thinking…'

'The blocks are big, if I remember correctly?'

'Don't forget, though, that Khmer temples are built without cement or foundations. They're like castles made out of dominoes.'

'Let's see, then: each domino, fifty square centimetres, a metre long… Seven hundred and fifty kilos approximately. Light, aren't they?'

'I thought of long saws, so that we only take away the carved side, without going too deep: impossible. I have hacksaws, which are faster. Above all, we'll have to hope that time has thrown almost everything to the ground, and that the fig trees and Siamese incendiaries have pretty effectively done the same job for us.'

'I've come across more fallen rocks than temples… And treasure hunters have also been through there… Until now, I never thought of the temples except in connection with them…'

Perken had raised his eyes from the map, and was looking at the light bulb; Claude wondered if he was thinking, for his gaze seemed distant, almost dreamy. 'What do I know of this man?' he thought once again, struck by that vacant face clearly silhouetted against the washbasin. The heavy, slow pounding of the engines hammered the silence, each blow urging this adversary to accept.

'Well?'

Perken pushed the map away and sat down on the bunk. 'All things considered, and putting aside objections, this plan of yours is feasible – I admit I wasn't thinking about that, I was dreaming of the moment I'd get hold of the money… I don't claim to attempt things which are sure to succeed: I pass on those. But let me make one thing clear, the only reason I'm accepting is because I have to go into Moi country.'

'Where?'

'Further to the north, but one thing doesn't exclude the other. I won't know exactly where I'm going until I get to Bangkok: I have to find – to look for – a man I used to like and mistrust in equal measure… The native militia have been investigating what they call his disappearance. In Bangkok, I'll be given their findings. I think…'

'So you accept?'

'Yes… that he set out for the region I've been dealing with. If he's dead I'll know what to expect. If not…'

'If not?'

'I'm not so keen on finding him… He'll spoil everything.'

He was jumping from one subject to the other so quickly that Claude found it hard to keep listening. So soon after accepting, the man did not exist. He looked in the direction of Perken's gaze: it was his, Claude's image, that he was staring at, in the mirror. For a moment, he saw his own forehead, his prominent chin, through another man's eyes. And this other man was thinking of him, too. 'Don't answer if you don't want to.' His eyes became sharper. 'Why are you attempting this?'

'I could answer: because I've almost run out of money, which is true.'

'There are other ways to make money. And why do you want it? It doesn't seem to be to enjoy it.'

'What about you?' thought Claude.

'When you're poor, it's difficult to choose your enemies,' he replied. 'I mistrust the small change of rebellion…'

Perken still had that look in his eyes, both intent and absent, as if focused on memories, which made Claude think of an intelligent priest. The eyes now took on a harder gleam. 'We never do anything with our lives.'

'But life does something with us.'

'Not always… What do you expect of yours?'

Claude did not reply at first. This man's past had been so totally transformed into experience, into barely suggested thought, into looks, that his actual life story ceased to matter. The only thing that remained between them – the only thing linking them – was whatever men had deep inside them. 'I think what I know above all is what I don't expect of it…'

'Each time you had to choose, you –'

'I'm not the one who chooses: it's whatever resists.'

'Resists what?'

He had asked himself this question so often, he was able to answer immediately. 'The awareness of death.'

'Decay is the real death.' Perken was now looking at his own face in the mirror. 'Ageing is so much worse than death! Accepting your fate, your function, the kennel you're forced to live in… You don't know what death is when you're young…'

And suddenly Claude realised what it was that linked him to this man who had accepted him without really understanding why: an obsession with death.

Perken took the map. 'I'll bring it back tomorrow.'

He shook Claude's hand and went out.

The atmosphere in the cabin closed over Claude again like the door of a dungeon. Perken's questions remained with him, like another prisoner. And his objections. No, there weren't so many ways to gain your freedom! He had reflected not so long ago – he was not naïve enough to be surprised – on the condition of a civilisation in which the mind mattered so little that those to whom it was the staple diet, who no doubt could eat their fill, were gradually led to make do with scraps. What to do, then? He had no desire to sell cars, stocks and shares, or speeches, like those of his friends whose slicked-down hair signified their distinction, nor to build bridges, like those whose badly cut hair signified their know-how. Why did such people work? To gain esteem. He hated the esteem they were seeking. For a man without children and without a god, submission to order was the most profound submission to death. You had to look for weapons where other people did not seek them. What the man who knew he was separate had to demand of himself before anything else was courage. What to do with the corpses of ideas which dominated the conduct of men who thought their existence was useful to some kind of salvation, what to do with the words – those other corpses – of those who wanted to live their lives according to a model? There was no purpose in life, but that in itself had become a condition of action. Let others confuse leaving everything to chance with attempting to predict the unknown. You had to rescue your own images from the stagnant world that kept them captive… 'What they call adventure,' he thought, 'isn't an escape, it's a hunt: the order of the world isn't destroyed to be replaced by chance, but simply out of a desire for profit.' He was familiar with those for whom adventure was a way of feeding their dreams – play the game, and you'll be able to dream – familiar, too, with the factor that made it possible for people to have hope. All that was paltry indeed. The austere desire to dominate he had spoken about to Perken, the desire to dominate death, echoed within him with every throb of the blood in his temples, as imperious as sexual need. It mattered little to him if he were killed, if he vanished off the face of the earth. He cared hardly at all for himself. That would be his struggle, even if not his victory. But to accept, while you were still alive, the futility of your own existence, like a cancer, to live with the clamminess of death on your hand… (Wasn't that the origin of the demand for eternal things, so heavily impregnated with its own smell of flesh?) What was this need for the unknown, this temporary destruction of the relations between prisoner and master, which those who didn't know it called adventure, if not a way of defending himself against death? The defence of a blind man, aiming to conquer death in order to raise the stakes...

To possess more than himself, to escape from the futile lives of the men he saw around him every day...

Perken had left the boat in Singapore to travel up to Bangkok. They had reached an agreement. Claude would join him in Phnom Penh, after getting his mission letter stamped in Saigon and visiting the French Institute. His being able to proceed would depend on coming to an arrangement with the Director of the Institute, who was hostile to initiatives like his.

One morning – the weather had worsened again – he saw, through the porthole of his cabin, some passengers pointing at some sort of spectacle. He rushed up on deck. Through a gap in the massed clouds, a pale sun shone down on the coast of Sumatra at the level of the restless sea. With the aid of binoculars, he looked at the monstrous foliage tumbling from the hill-tops all the way down to the shore, bristling here and there with palms, black in the colourless expanse. Here and there in the distance, above the ridges, there shone pale fires, from which thick smoke rose. Lower down, tree ferns stood out clearly against the masses of shadow. He could not take his eyes off these swathes of plant life. How to find your way through such vegetation? Others had done it, he could too. But this nervous assertion was silently answered by the low sky and the inextricable tissue of leaves crawling with insects...

He went back to his cabin. His plan, as long as he had carried it alone, had detached him from the world, restricting him to an incommunicable universe like that of a blind man or a lunatic, a universe in which the jungle and the monuments gradually came to life whenever his attention flagged, as hostile as large animals... The presence of Perken had brought everything back to a human level, but now he was sinking again, tense but clear-headed, into his addictive obsession. He opened his book at the pages he had marked: *The ornamental motifs have been badly damaged by the constant dampness of the undergrowth and the heavy rainfall... the vault has collapsed completely... There are almost certainly other monuments in this now virtually deserted region, dotted with jungle clearings through which herds of elephants and wild buffalo roam... The interiors of the galleries are impossibly cluttered with fallen blocks of sandstone which once formed the vaults: this particularly deplorable state of dilapidation seems due to the use of wood in the construction... The tall trees which have grown in places over the rubble now jut over the tops of the walls, and their roots have become inextricably tangled... The country is almost deserted...* What could he use to fight this battle? As the noise of the engines increased, he tried to shake off the two words 'French Institute, French Institute, French Institute', which buzzed in his head like a saw. 'I know those people,' Perken had said, 'you're not one of them.' Obviously. He would be careful. He knew, though, that men are good at recognising those who reject the things they accept, that the atheist was much more scandalous now that faith no longer existed. His grandfather's whole life had taught him that. These people had two-thirds of what he needed...

To free himself from a life given over to hopes and dreams, to escape the inertia of this ship!

3

In front of a window, its square of light framing a few palms and a wall made green, almost blue, by tropical rains, Albert Ramèges, director of the French Institute, smoothed his chestnut beard with his hand and watched as Monsieur Vannec came in.

'The Minister for Colonies informed us you were on your way, monsieur, so I was pleased to receive your phone call yesterday and learn that you had arrived. It goes without saying that if we can be useful to you in any way, we are at your disposal. If you need... advice, you can expect the warmest consideration from all my colleagues here. We can finalise all that later.'

He walked away from his desk and came and sat down next to Claude. 'The consideration begins,' Claude thought.

'I am happy to see you here, monsieur,' the director said, his tone already more familiar. 'I read carefully the interesting articles on Asian art that you published last year. I've also read your theories – not until I knew you had arrived, I confess. I must say that I was more attracted than convinced by the arguments you put forward, but I was genuinely interested. You belong to a generation that is full of curiosity...'

'I put forward these ideas in order to...' – 'to clear the ground', he thought, and hesitated – 'to be free to develop another idea which interests me more...'

Ramèges was looking at him questioningly. Claude was keenly aware that the man was eager not to be confused with his official position, to show that he was superior to it, to receive him like a guest – boredom no doubt had something to do with it, and perhaps a certain esprit de corps. But he was also aware that archaeologists with philological training were absurdly hostile to all others. Ramèges's dreams were centred on the Institute. Impossible to broach the subject of his mission straight away: it would have hurt the man as surely as if he had insulted him.

'What I mean is that the essential value we place on the artist conceals from us one of the most important aspects in the life of the work of art: the state of the civilisation that contemplates it. It is as if in art time does not exist. What interests me, you see, is the way these works are broken down and transformed, their innermost lives, made up of the deaths of men. Every work of art, in short, has a tendency to become a myth.'

He felt that he was condensing his ideas too much, and in so doing rendering them obscure. He was hampered by the desire to get to the object of his visit, but also to win over Ramèges, who was lost in thought, clearly intrigued. The sound of the heavy drops falling outside entered the room.

'Be that as it may, it's curious…'

'For me, museums are places where the works of the past, which have become myths, sleep – live their historical lives – waiting for artists to summon them back to real life. And the reason they touch me directly is that the artist has the power of resurrection… No civilisation can ever be completely under-stood by another. But the objects remain, and we are blind to them until our myths are in harmony with them…'

Ramèges continued to smile, curious and attentive. 'He thinks I'm just a theorist,' Claude thought. 'He's pale, most likely a liver abscess: he'd understand me so much more easily if he realised that what really interests me is man's determination to defend himself against his own death through this turbulent sense of eternity, if I linked what I'm saying to his abscess! But never mind…' He smiled in his turn, and this smile, which Ramèges attributed to the desire to be pleasant to him, estab-lished a certain cordiality between them.

'When it comes down to it,' the director said at last, 'you don't trust anyone, that's the truth, you don't trust anyone... Oh, I know perfectly well, it isn't always easy... Look at this piece of pottery, here, under this book. It was sent from Tien Tsin. The designs are Greek, definitely ancient: sixth century BC at least. And there's a Chinese dragon on the shield! So many of our ideas about the relations between Europe and Asia before the Christian era need revising! But what can we do? When science tells us we have been mistaken, we have to start again...'

Claude felt closer to Ramèges now, because of the sadness with which he spoke. Had these discoveries forced him to abandon something he had been working on for a long time? To save face, Claude looked at other photos, some of Khmer statues, the others of Cham statues, divided into two series. To break the silence that had fallen, he pointed to the two packets and asked, 'Which do you prefer?'

'I have no preferences. I'm an archaeologist...' 'I've got over such tastes,' his tone implied, 'such youthful innocence...' He sensed a climbdown, which annoyed him somewhat: even when he was not asking questions, he meant to call the tune. 'To get back to your plans, monsieur. Your intention, if I'm not mistaken, is to follow the route of the old Khmer royal road...'

Claude nodded.

'I must tell you first of all that large sections of the trail – I'm not even talking about the road – are invisible. As you approach the Dang Rek mountain range, it disappears completely.'

'I'll find it again,' Claude replied, with a smile.

'I sincerely hope so... It is my duty – and my function – to warn you of the dangers you will face. I am sure you know that two of our representatives, Henri Maître and Odend'hal, were murdered. And yet our unfortunate friends knew the country well.'

'I'm sure it won't surprise you, monsieur, when I tell you that I'm not looking for an easy life. May I ask what help you can put at my disposal?'

'You'll receive requisition vouchers which will enable you to obtain, through the Resident, as is only proper, the Cambodian carts necessary for transporting your luggage and their drivers. Fortunately, the things an expedition like yours transports are relatively light...'

'Are the stones light?'

'In order to prevent any repetition of the unfortunate abuses that occurred last year, it has been decided that all objects, whatever their nature, should remain in situ.'

'I beg your pardon?'

'In situ: in place. A report will be made. Once we've examined this report, the head of our archaeological service, if he deems it necessary, will visit...'

'After what you've told me, it seems quite unlikely to me that the head of your archaeological service will take the risk of entering the regions I'm going through...'

'This is a special case: we'll think about it.'

'And even if he took the risk, I'd like to know why I should play the prospector so that he can benefit.'

'Do you prefer to play it so that you alone can benefit?' Ramèges asked softly.

'In twenty years, your services haven't explored that region. I'm sure they had better things to do. But I know what I'm risking, and I want to risk it without orders.'

'But not without help?'

They were both talking slowly, without raising their voices. Claude was struggling with the rage that swept over him: what gave this functionary rights over objects which he, Claude, might discover, the very objects he had come all this way to find, the objects that represented his last hope?

'With no other help than what I've been promised. With less help than you give a geographical officer to go through a region which is under your control.'

'You're surely not expecting the administration, monsieur, to provide you with a military escort?'

'Have I asked for anything other than what you yourself proposed: the means to requisition carts and drivers, since there's no other way of proceeding?'

Ramèges looked at him in silence. After an awkward pause, Claude was expecting to hear the sound of rain outside, but the downpour had stopped.

'There are two possibilities,' he continued. 'Either I don't come back, and there's nothing more to say. Or I come back, and whatever profit I make, it will be derisory in comparison with the results I bring with me.'

'Bring for whom?'

'I shan't insult you, monsieur, by thinking that you're determined not to accept any contribution to the history of art which hasn't come from your Institute.'

'The value of these contributions is all too dependent, alas, on the technical training, the experience, the discipline of those who make them...'

'The spirit of discipline doesn't lead to rebel country.'

'But the spirit which does lead to rebel country...' Ramèges left the sentence unfinished, and stood up. 'Anyway, monsieur, it is my duty to help you in specific ways. You may rest assured that I shall. As for the rest...'

'As for the rest...' Claude made a gesture which meant, as discreetly as possible, 'I'll take care of it.'

'When are you planning to leave?'

'As soon as possible.'

'In that case, you'll have your documents by tomorrow evening.'

With great courtesy, the director walked him to the door.

'Let's sum up,' Claude said to himself as he crossed the courtyard, but then, as if to escape his own injunction, gazed at the fragments of gods over which night lizards were running. 'Let's sum up.'

He couldn't do it. He turned into the deserted boulevard. The word 'colony' haunted him with the plaintive resonance it had in the ballads of the Islands. Cats passed furtively along the ditches... 'That bearded worthy doesn't want anyone poaching on his territory...' He was beginning to realise, though, that Ramèges was not motivated by self interest, as he had thought at first. He was defending order, not so much against a plan as against a temperament so diametrically opposed to his... And he was defending the prestige of his Institute. 'Even from his own point of view, he ought to try and get what he can from me. It's obvious the people he has working for him now won't risk their skins up there. He's acting like an administrator who's building up his reserves: in thirty years perhaps... Will his Institute still be here in thirty years, and will the French still be in Indochina? He probably even thinks that the only reason his representatives died was so that his colleagues should continue their work, even though neither of them died for his Institute... If he's defending a collective, he'll become aggressive. If he thinks he's defending the dead, he'll become fanatical. We'll have to try and predict what he's going to dream up next...'

4

Against the window of the launch that would carry them to land, Claude saw Perken's profile again, as he had so often seen it, at mealtimes, against the ship's porthole. At the rear, the white boat that had brought them from Pnom-Penh during the night was moored. The area where Perken's former comrade had vanished was not far from the Way of the Kings, which virtually marked the boundary of rebel country, and the information he had cautiously obtained in Bangkok had confirmed the value of Claude's plan.

The launch set sail, plunging into the submerged trees. The branches that brushed against the windows were covered in mud coagulated by the heat and vertical strands of silt. On the trunks, rings of dried foam marked the furthest height the water reached. Claude gazed with fascination at this foretaste of the jungle that awaited him, overwhelmed by the smell of the silt spreading slowly in the sun, the insipid foam drying, the animals rotting, the limp appearance of the mud-coloured amphibians clinging to the branches. Every time there was a gap in the leaves, he tried to glimpse the towers of Angkor Wat against the trees twisting in the wind from the lake, but in vain: the leaves, red with twilight, closed again over this malarial life. The fetidness reminded him of a blind man he had seen in Phnom Penh, chanting the Ramayana in the middle of a pitiful circle, to the accompaniment of a rough guitar. There was a connection between that old man, who no longer roused anyone with his heroic poem but a circle of beggars and servant girls, and this decaying Cambodia: a tamed earth, a domesticated earth, where the hymns were as much in ruins as the temples, a dead earth among the dead. And these filthy molluscs gurgling in their shells, like foul crickets… Ahead of him the enemy, the earthbound jungle, like a clenched fist.

The launch finally reached land. The Fords from the rental service were waiting for the travellers. A native left the group and walked up to the captain.

'This is the fellow,' the captain said to Claude.

'The boy?'

'I'm not sure he's all that wonderful, but he's the only one in Siem Reap.'

Perken asked the boy a few of the usual questions, and hired him.

'Whatever you do, don't give him an advance,' the captain cried, as he walked away.

The native gave a slight shrug of the shoulders and took his place beside the driver of the white men's car, which left immediately. Another car was transporting the luggage.

'Bungalow?' the driver asked, without turning round. The car was already speeding along the straight road.

'No, the Residence first.'

The jungle flew past on either side of the red road, against which the boy's shaven head stood out. The screeching of the cicadas was so shrill, it could be heard over the noise of the engine. Suddenly, the driver stretched out his arm towards the horizon, which had appeared for a moment: 'Angkor Wat.' But Claude could see no further than twenty metres.

Finally fires and lanterns appeared, flecked with the silhouettes of hens and black pigs: the village. Before long, the car came to a halt.

'The Residence?'

'Yes, Mssié.'

'I don't suppose I'll be long,' Claude said to Perken.

The Resident was waiting for him in a high-ceilinged room. He walked up to him and slowly shook his hand, as if weighing it. 'Pleased to see you, Monsieur Vannec, pleased to see you... Been waiting quite a while... Damned boat late as usual...'

The man grunted his words of welcome into his thick white moustache, without letting go of Claude's hand. The shadow of his firm nose, projected on the whitewashed wall, cut the corner off a Cambodian painting.

'So, you want to go into the jungle, eh? Just like that?'

'Since you've been informed of my coming, monsieur, I'm sure you know precisely what mission I'm about to undertake.'

'About to undertake, eh? About to undertake… Well, that's your affair.'

'I assume I can count on your help to carry out the necessary requisitions before my caravan leaves?'

The old Resident stood up without replying: his old joints cracked in the silence. He began to walk across the room, followed by his shadow. 'Have to walk, Monsieur Vannec, if you don't want to be eaten by these damned mosquitoes… This is a bad hour of the day, as you know… Requisitions… hmm!'

('I can't stand the way he keeps clearing his throat,' thought Claude. 'Enough of playing the senile old general!') 'The requisitions?' he said.

'Well, there you are, you see… You'll get them of course… Only, you know, they don't amount to much. I know perfectly well that you fellows who come here don't like to feel you're being lectured to, it annoys you… but all the same…'

'Go on.'

'What you're planning isn't a little stroll like the others have done. So there's one thing I have to tell you. In this country, requisitions, well, it's just like saying: don't forget your skin.'

'You mean I won't get anything?'

'Oh, no, that's not what I mean. You have a mission, you have a mission, no one can do anything about that. We'll give you what we have to give you. You may not think it's as good as it ought to be, but you'll get it. You can rest easy on that score. Instructions are instructions. '

'Meaning what?'

'I'm sure you're not expecting me to confide in you. But, the fact is, there are things in this damned job I don't always like. I don't like trouble. So there is something I'd like to tell you, something important, call it advice if you like! Monsieur Vannec, you mustn't go into the jungle. Drop the idea, it's more sensible. Go back to a big city, Saigon, for example. And wait a bit. Trust me.'

'Do you think I've come halfway round the world to then just saunter off to Saigon looking pleased with myself?'

'All of us here have come halfway round the world, it's nothing to boast of... But precisely because you made so much effort, couldn't you have arranged something with Monsieur Ramèges and – what do you call it – his Institute? It would have been better for everyone, and I wouldn't have had to get involved in any trouble... All I can say is –'

'On the one hand, monsieur, you're giving me this advice, because it seems you have a certain sympathy for me' (he almost added, 'or a certain antipathy to the French Institute', but said nothing) 'and on the other hand, you're telling me that whatever happens I won't be prevented from attempting my mission: I find it hard to –'

'I didn't say that. I said you will be given what you are entitled to...'

'Oh yes... I think I'm starting to understand. But all the same I'd like to –'

'Know more? Well, you have to realise that's a wish that won't be granted. Now, let's be practical. Do you want to think it over?'

'No.'

'You're determined to leave?'

'Definitely.'

'Good. Let's hope you have good reasons, because if you didn't, Monsieur Vannec, without wishing to offend you, you'd be making a big mistake. Talking of which, I need to give you... no, that can wait... well, anyway, I must say something about Monsieur Perken.'

'What?'

'I have here… wait, it must be in the other file… well, it doesn't matter… I have here somewhere a note from the Cambodian security forces, of which I've been asked to "give you the gist". Let's be clear about this: I'm only telling you what I'm about to tell you because I've been asked to. Because, you know, I hate that kind of thing. It's ridiculous. The one serious problem in the region is the trade in wood. They'd be better off helping me do my job properly than boring me to tears with stories of rocks and stones.'

'Well?'

'Well, this fellow Perken who's going with you has been given his travelling papers at the insistence of the Siamese government. He's supposed to be looking for a man named Grabot – or so he says! We could have refused, mark you, because as far as we're concerned, this Grabot is a deserter…'

'So why didn't you refuse? Surely not out of the goodness of your hearts?'

'If someone disappears here, we have to get to the bottom of it. This Grabot's just a thug. And more likely to have been on the coast when he left.'

'I don't think Perken knew him very well, but what's it to do with me?'

'Perken is something high up in the Siamese government, isn't he, even though he's not very official. I know him: I've been hearing about him for ten years now. And let me tell you this, just between you and me: before he left for Europe, he was negotiating with us – with us, mind, not with the Siamese – for the purchase of a few machine guns.'

Claude looked at the Resident in silence.

'So, Monsieur Vannec, that's the way it is. Now – when do you want to leave?'

'As soon as possible.'

'In three days, then. You'll get what you need at six in the morning. Do you have a boy?'

'Yes, he's in the car.'

'I'll go down with you. I need to give him his instructions right away. Oh, by the way, your letters!'

He handed Claude a number of envelopes. One bore the letterhead of the French Institute. Claude was about to open it, but the tone in which the Resident was calling his boy made him look up. The car was waiting, looking blue in the light from the bulb over the door. The boy, who had moved aside – no doubt on seeing the Resident appear – came forward, hesitantly. They exchanged a few words in Annamite: understanding nothing, Claude watched all the more attentively. The boy seemed dismayed. The Resident was gesticulating, his white moustache shiny with electric light.

'I warn you, this boy is just out of prison.'

'What was he in for?'

'Gambling, petty thieving. You ought to get another.'

'I'll see.'

'Well, I brought him up to date. If you replace him, he'll hand on my instructions…'

The Resident said something else in Annamite, then shook Claude's hand, looking him in the eyes, half-opening his mouth and closing it again, as if he were about to say something more. His body remained motionless, clear against the dark background of the jungle, from his close-cropped white hair to his canvas shoes. He did not relax his grip. 'Does he have something to tell me?' Claude wondered. But the Resident let go of his hand, turned, and with a last 'Hmmm!' followed by some mumbled words, went back inside.

'Boy?'

'Mssié?'

'What's your name?'

'Xa.'

'Did you hear what the Resident said about you?'

'Not true, Mssié!'

'I don't care whether it's true or not. Do you hear me? I don't care. If you do what I ask, I don't give a damn about the rest. Understood?'

The boy looked at Claude in surprise.

'Understood?'

'Yes, Mssié…'

'Good. And did you also hear what the captain said?'

' "Not give advance." '

'Here are five piastres. Driver, let's go.'

He took his seat again.

'Is that your method?' Perken asked with a smile.

'You could call it that. If he's a rogue, we won't see him again tomorrow. If not, we've got him on our side. Loyalty is one of the few sentiments which don't seem to me have gone rotten…'

'Perhaps… So what did that grouchy old soldier have to say?'

Claude reflected. 'Some curious things, which I need to talk to you about. But let's sum up first. We'll have our carts the day after tomorrow. He makes no bones about the fact that he thinks I'd be wise to go back to Saigon…'

'Why?'

'He doesn't say… He intends to follow the instructions he's been given, even though, as far as one can see, he thinks they're a terrible nuisance.'

'Weren't you able to find out any more?'

'No… Unless… Wait… wait…'

He still had the envelope in his hand. He had difficulty opening it, and when he had unfolded the letter, he could not read it. Perken took out his torch.

'Stop!' Claude called.

The noise of the engine subsided, and was swallowed by the screeching of the cicadas.

' "*Dear Monsieur*," ' Claude read aloud, ' "*I believe it is my duty*" – that's a good start – "*in order to avoid confusion, and to enable you to keep the necessary watch over the people likely to accompany you – to convey to you the enclosed order of the Governor General, an order which is still valid. I am sorry if anything in it seems unclear, I shall be sending you details this week of the latest decisions by the administration.*

' "*Please rest assured*" – oh, never mind all that... – "*that I wish you the very best of luck. Yours sincerely.*" (What order?)'

He took the second sheet:

' "*The Governor General of Indochina, at the suggestion of the Director of the French Institute...*" – never mind, damn it! – "*decrees:*

' "*That all monuments so far discovered or yet to be discovered within the territory of the provinces of Siam Reap, Battambong and Sisophon are hereby declared historical monuments...*" This is from 1908.'

'Does it go on?'

'Administrative stuff: a pity we stopped on such a fine road for this! Driver, carry on!'

'Well?' Perken was now shining the torch in his face.

'Turn that off, will you? What do you mean, well? You don't think this is going to change my mind, do you?'

'I'm glad I was right to think it won't change your mind. I was expecting this kind of reaction from the administration, I told you that on the boat. It'll be more difficult, that's all. But in the jungle...'

It was so clear to Claude that there was no possibility of going back that the thought of discussing what he was going to do exasperated him. The game was beginning: so much the better. He dismissed his anxieties: they had to keep moving forward, like this car which was plunging into the black air, the shapeless jungle. The shadowy figure of a horse appeared fleetingly in the headlights, then electric lights came into view…

The bungalow.

The boy busied himself with the luggage. Even before asking for a drink, Claude moved aside the yellowed issues of *L'Illustration* on the rattan table and, ignoring the buzzing of the mosquitoes, unscrewed the cap of his pen.

'You're not going to reply now?'

'Don't worry, I won't send the letter until we leave. But I am going to reply, it'll calm my nerves. In any case, I'll keep it short.'

Just two lines, in fact. While he wrote the address, he passed the sheet of paper to Perken.

Dear Monsieur

   The skin of the bear is also considered a historical monument, but it might be unwise to go looking for it.

Even more sincerely,
– Claude Vannec

The boy attending to the bungalow was bringing the sodas unasked. 'Let's drink and go out,' said Claude. 'There's more.'

The great roadway of Angkor Wat began opposite the bungalow. They started along it, twisting their feet at every step on the loose paving stones.

Perken sat down on a stone. 'Well?'

Claude told him about the conversation he had had with the Resident. Perken lit a cigarette: his face, quite close to the flame of the lighter, emerged for a second from the darkness, wrinkled and scarred, before melting into the reddish gleam of the lighted tobacco…

'Did the Resident say anything more about me?'

'That was more than enough…'

'And what did you think of it all?'

'Nothing. We're risking our lives together: I'm here to help you, not to hold you to account. If you need machine guns, I'm only sorry you didn't tell me, because I'd like to find some for you.'

The vast silence of the jungle descended again, tasting of freshly turned earth. The raucous cry of a cane toad – so much like the squeal of a pig having its throat cut – suddenly filled it, and at once disappeared in the darkness and the smell of ponds…

'You have to realise this. When I accept a man, I accept him totally, I accept him as I accept myself. Is there any act this man who is one of my people could have committed that I can honestly state I wouldn't have committed myself ?'

Silence again.

'Haven't you ever been seriously betrayed?'

'You don't think differently from the mass of men without running risks. But who would I turn to, if not those who defend themselves as I do?'

'Or attack…'

'Or attack.'

'And you don't care where this friendship might lead you?'

'Should I be afraid of making love because of the pox? I don't say: I don't care. I say: I accept it.' In the darkness, Perken placed his hand on Claude's shoulder. 'I hope you die young, Claude, as I have hoped for few things in this world… You have no idea what it is to be a prisoner of your own life: I didn't begin to realise it myself until Sarah and I parted. I didn't care that she slept with any man she was attracted to – especially when she was on her own – she would have followed me to jail, and she'd been through many things in Siam since she married Prince

Pitsanulok… A woman who knew a lot about life, but nothing about death. One day she saw that her life had taken on a shape that was mine, that her destiny lay there and not anywhere else, and she began to look at me with as much hatred as when she looked in her mirror… You know the way white women look in their mirrors and realise they're always going to have that flushed complexion they acquired in the Tropics… All the hopes she'd had as a young woman began to eat away at her life like a bout of syphilis caught in adolescence – and the contagion spread to my life, too… You have no idea what it's like, to know your destiny is limited and inevitable, you're like a convict being read the prison rules: the certainty that you will be this and not something else, that you *will have been* that and not something else, that what you haven't had, you'll never have. And all your hopes are in the past, but you still have them under your skin in a way you'll never have another living being…'

The decaying smell of the ponds enveloped Claude, who saw again his mother wandering through his grandfather's mansion: almost hidden in the gloom, except for the scroll of her heavy hair reflecting the daylight, looking with horror, in the little mirror decorated with a romantic galleon, at the way the corners of her mouth had collapsed and her nose was getting bigger, massaging her eyelids like a blind woman…

'I understood,' Perken went on, 'because I myself wasn't so far away from the moment when I would have to settle accounts with my own hopes. It was as if we had to kill someone we'd been living for. As simple and as merry as that. More words you probably don't know the meaning of: to kill someone who doesn't want to die… And when you don't have children, when you never wanted children, your hopes can't be passed on, you can't give them to anyone, you really have to kill them yourself. That's why you can feel such an affinity when you come across it in others…'

Like a note repeated from one octave to another, the cries of frogs spread through the darkness all the way to the unseen horizon.

'Youth is a religion you always have to be converted from in the end... And yet!... I tried seriously to do what Mayrena was hoping for when he imagined himself strutting about on the stage of a French theatre. To be a king is foolish; what matters is to build a kingdom. I didn't play the fool with a sabre. I barely used my rifle – though I'm a good shot, believe me. But I'm connected, in one way or another, with almost all the chiefs of the free tribes from here to Upper Laos. That's been going on for fifteen years. I got to them one by one, whether they were idiots or brave men. They don't know the Siamese, they know me.'

'What do you want to do with them?'

'I *wanted*... A military force, first. Rough and ready, but capable of being transformed quickly. And then to wait for the inevitable conflict in these parts, either between colonists and coloniscd, or just among colonists. Then you could really play the game. With a large number of men, perhaps for a long time. I want to leave a scar on this map. If I have to gamble against my own death, I prefer to gamble with twenty tribes rather than with a child... I wanted that the way my father wanted his neighbour's property, the way I want women.'

The tone surprised Claude. This wasn't the voice of a man obsessed: it was rigorous and premeditated.

'Why don't you want it any more?'

'Because I want peace.'

He said: peace, as he might have said: action. Although his cigarette was alight, he had not extinguished his lighter. He moved it closer to the wall, and looked carefully at the carvings and the line separating the stones. It was as if he was seeking his peace there.

'You'd never be able to carry anything away from a wall like this.'

He finally extinguished the little flame. The wall was again plunged into an intense darkness barely disturbed by lights above their heads – most likely sticks of lighted incense in front of the Buddhas. Half the stars were hidden by the huge, solid mass before them, which asserted itself, although invisible, simply by its presence in the shadows.

'Can you smell the silt?' Perken resumed. 'My plan is just as rotten. I don't have any more time. Within two years, they'll have finished extending the railway lines. Within five years, there'll be roads and trains all over the bush.'

'Is it the strategic value of the roads that worries you?'

'They don't have any. But with alcohol and cheap trash flooding in, my Mois will be done for. There's nothing I can do about it. I have to hand over to the Siamese or else give up.'

'What about the machine guns?'

'In my own territory, I'm free. If I'm armed, I'll hold on there until I die. And there are the women. With a few machine guns, we can hold out against the government. They can't take it unless they're ready to sacrifice a lot of men.'

Were the still unfinished railway lines enough to justify his words? It wasn't very likely that the rebel country could hold out against 'civilisation', against the Annamites and Siamese who were its advance guard. 'The women…' Claude had not forgotten Djibouti.

'Is it only because you've thought it through that you've abandoned your plan?'

'I haven't abandoned it: if the opportunity… But I don't want it to be the main thing I live for any more. I've thought about it a lot, especially since the fiasco in the brothel in Djibouti… You see, I think what made me abandon it, as you put it, were the women I haven't had. It isn't impotence, you understand. It's a threat… Like the first time I realised Sarah was getting older. The *end* of something, above all… I feel drained of hope, and the force of that is rising inside me, against me – like hunger.'

He was aware of the discreet contact these hammered words maintained between Claude and him.

'I've always been indifferent to money. The Siamese owe me more than I'd ask them for, but they won't play ball. They don't trust me… Not that there's any particular reason: they just don't trust me, full stop, just as I don't trust the two or three years I'm being forced to keep my hopes on hold… We ought to attempt these things without relying on governments, otherwise we're like hunting dogs who have to wait before they can hunt for themselves. But no one has ever pulled it off – in fact no one has ever tried it seriously. Brooke in Sarawak, even Mayrena… Schemes like theirs are mad when you think what they cost. If I've gambled my life on a game that's bigger than me…'

'What else can you do?'

'Nothing. But this game concealed the rest of the world from me, and sometimes I have a strange need for it to be hidden… If I'd realised my plan… But even if everything I think is nonsense, I don't care, because there are the women.'

'Their bodies?'

'You have no idea how much hatred of the world there is in that: always wanting one more. Any body you haven't possessed is an enemy… Now all my old dreams are in my loins…'

His desire to convince weighed close and heavy on Claude, like the temple hidden in the darkness.

'You have to realise what this country is. I'm only now starting to understand their erotic cults, this idea that a man is able to merge, in sensation, with the woman he possesses, to imagine he is *her* without ceasing to be himself. Nothing can equal the sensual pleasure of someone who realises he can't bear pleasure any more. No, they aren't bodies, these women: they are… yes, possibilities. And I want…'

He made a gesture which Claude could barely make out in the darkness, like a hand crushing something.

'…just as I wanted to dominate men.'

'What he wants,' thought Claude, 'is to destroy himself. Does he realise that more than he's letting on? He'll do it, too…' Perken had spoken of his dashed hopes in a tone that made it hard to believe he had abandoned them: or if he had, sex was not the only compensation.

'I haven't yet finished with men… From where I'm going, I'll still be able to keep an eye on the Mekong – a pity I don't know the region where we're going, or that you don't know a Way of the Kings three hundred kilometres further north! But I intend to keep an eye on it alone, without any neighbours. We have to see what's become of Grabot…'

'Where did he go?'

'Very close to the Dang Reks, about fifty kilometres off our planned route. To do what? His chums in Bangkok say he's after gold: all the flotsam and jetsam of Europe are always thinking about gold. But he knows the country: he's not interested in that kind of nonsense. I was also told about a scheme to sell objects to the rebel tribes for barter…'

'How do they pay?'

'In skins, sometimes in gold powder. A scheme like that is more likely. He's a Parisian: his father is said to have invented tie holders, car starters, tap swirls… I think the main reason he went was to settle accounts with himself… I'll tell you about him one day. But I'm sure he left with the agreement of the government in Bangkok: why else would they be so keen to get him back? My guess is, he went there for them and now he's starting to play his own game – a bit premature, in my opinion – otherwise, he would have been in touch with them. Maybe they'd asked him to check on my situation up there. It was while I was away that he left…'

'But he didn't go to the same region as you?'

'If he had, he'd have been greeted with arrows, and especially a few bullets from the rifles I use for training. It's useless trying. The only way he could have gone – if that was where he was going – is across the Dang Reks.'

'What kind of man is he?'

'Listen to this. During his military service, he took a real dislike to a doctor – a major – who hadn't accepted that he was ill, I think, or for some other reason. He has himself taken ill again the following week, goes to the infirmary: "You again?" "Spots." "Where?" He opens his hand and says, "Spot them!" He's sentenced to a month in prison. He immediately writes to the general, tells him he has an eye disease. As soon as he gets into prison – I forgot to tell you he had gonorrhoea – he takes some pus from the gonorrhoea, knowing perfectly well what he's doing, and sticks it in his eye. The major gets punished, but Grabot loses his eye, of course. He's one-eyed. One of your very round French faces, a potato-shaped nose, a body like a removal man. A big brute of a fellow. In the bars of Bangkok, he loved to make a casual entry. Picture it: everyone giving him sidelong looks, men gradually making way for him, some chums of his in a corner – not many – raising their glasses and yelling… He was a fugitive from one of your African battalions. Another man with an unusual attitude to eroticism…'

Part Two

I

For four days now, the jungle.

For four days, making camp near villages that grew out of the jungle, like their wooden Buddhas, like the palm thatch on their huts, emerging from the soft ground like monstrous insects: the mind breaking down in this aquarium light, as thick as water. They had already come across a number of squat monuments, their stones held to the ground so tightly, by roots clutching them like paws, that they no longer seemed to have been raised by men but by long-extinct creatures accustomed to this life without a horizon, this underwater gloom. Over the centuries, the Way had disintegrated, and only revealed its presence in these massive, rotting structures, the eyes of some toad motionless in a corner of the stones. Did these monuments, abandoned by the jungle like skeletons, hold a promise or a rejection? Was the caravan ever going to reach the carved temple towards which it was being guided by an adolescent chain-smoking Perken's cigarettes? They should have been there three hours ago... The jungle and the heat, though, were stronger than their anxiety: like a man sinking into an illness, Claude was sinking into this ferment, in which the shapes swelled and grew and decayed outside the world where men mattered, dividing him from himself with the force of darkness. And everywhere, insects.

The other animals, furtive, usually invisible, came from another universe, a universe in which the leaves on the trees did not seem joined by the air itself to the gummy leaves over which the horses walked, a universe that appeared occasionally in the violent shafts of sunlight, the whirl of sparkling atoms through which the shadows of birds passed in a flash. But the insects lived off the jungle, from the little black creatures, round as balls, crushed by the hooves of the bullocks pulling the carts and the ants scurrying up the sides of the porous trees, to the spiders held by their grasshopper legs in the centres of webs four metres across, the threads of which gathered the daylight that still lingered near the ground and appeared from a distance, in this profusion of phosphorescent and geometric forms, to be forever motionless. They alone, amid all the mollusc-like movement of the bush, seemed fixed, and only a dubious analogy linked them to the other insects: the cockroaches, the flies, the nameless creatures whose heads emerged from their shells at the level of the moss, the disgusting virulence of microscopic life. The high, whitish termites' nests, on top of which no termites were ever to be seen, rose in the gloom like abandoned planets, as if born out of the corrupt air, the fungus smell, the presence of tiny leeches clustered together beneath the leaves like flies' eggs. The unity of the jungle was asserting itself now. For the past six days Claude had given up trying to separate the creatures from the shapes, the life that moved from the life that oozed. An unknown power linked the fungus and the trees, made all these fleeting things swarm on this marshlike soil, in these steaming, primeval woods. What human action had any meaning here? Whose will retained any force? Everything spread, grew soft, made an effort to adapt to this world which was revolting and attractive at the same time, like the look on an idiot's face, a world that attacked the nerves with the same despicable power as those spiders hanging from the branches, from which he had found it so difficult to turn away his eyes.

The horses walked with their necks bowed, in silence. The young guide advanced slowly, but unhesitatingly, followed by a Cambodian called Svay, whom the Resident had attached to the caravan to requisition the drivers – and to keep an eye on things. Just as Claude was turning his head, as quickly as possible – his morbid fear of walking into a spider's web obliged him to look carefully in front of him – he jumped: Perken had just touched his arm, indicating with his cigarette, so red in the dark air, a form buried among the trees, from which here and there reeds emerged. Once again, Claude had been unable to distinguish anything through the tree trunks. He approached the vestiges of a brown stone wall flecked with moss and glistening with a few little pearls of dew that had not yet evaporated… 'The perimeter,' he thought. 'The ditch has been filled in.'

The path disappeared beneath their feet. They walked around the mass of fallen rocks. On the other side, a profusion of reeds, intertwined like a trellis, barred the jungle at a man's height.

The boy shouted to the drivers of the carts to bring their machetes: a sluggish voice, crushed beneath the vault of leaves… Claude's half-tensed hands recalled other digs, the hammer searching for an unknown object through the layer of earth. The drivers' torsos bent in a slow, almost lazy movement and immediately straightened up again, surmounted by the blue iron of the machetes reflecting the brightness of the invisible sky as they swung. With each parallel movement of the implements, from right to left, Claude felt in his arm the needle wielded by a doctor who had once scratched his skin while clumsily looking for a vein. From the gradually widening path rose a marshy smell, sicklier than that of the jungle. Perken was following the drivers step by step. Beneath his leather shoes, a reed, long dead no doubt, snapped with a dry sound. Two frogs fled unhurriedly from the ruins.

Above the trees, large birds flew away heavily. In their reaping, the drivers had reached a wall. The easiest thing to do was to find the gate, and find their way from there: they could only have drifted to the left, so what they had to do now was follow the wall to the right. Reeds and prickly shrubs grew right up to the foot of the wall. Claude hoisted himself up until he stood on the top.

'Can you move forward?' Perken asked.

The wall cut across the vegetation like a path, but it was covered with sticky moss. If Claude tried to walk along the top, the fall would be extremely dangerous: gangrene is as much the master of the jungle as the insect. He began to move forward on his stomach. The moss smelled of decay, and was covered in leaves that were half viscous and half reduced to their veins, as if partly digested. So close to his face, the moss looked very big – he could see the fibrils stirring slightly in the calm air – and he was reminded, too, that there were insects here. After three metres, he felt a tickling sensation.

He stopped, and scratched his neck. The tickling moved over his hand, and he pulled it away immediately: two black ants as big as wasps, their antennae distinctly visible, were trying to slip between his fingers. He shook his hand as hard as he could, and they fell. He was already on his feet. No ants on his clothes. At the end of the wall, a hundred metres away, a brighter gap: that had to be the gate, and the carvings. Below, the earth, covered in fallen stones. Against the bright gap, the silhouette of a branch: large ants, their bellies in silhouette too, their feet invisible, crossed it like a bridge. Claude tried to push it away, but he missed it at first. 'I absolutely have to get to the end. If there are red ants, it'll be bad, but if I go back it'll be worse… Unless they've exaggerated?'

'Well?' Perken cried.

He did not reply, took another step forward. It was difficult to find his balance. The wall drew his hands with the strength of a living creature. He collapsed onto it, and all at once, his muscles told him how he should walk: not on his hands and knees, but on his hands and toes, his back curved like a cat. He immediately advanced. Each hand could protect the other, while his feet and calves were protected by the leather, their contact with the moss reduced to the minimum. 'I'm fine!' he cried. He was surprised by the harsh, discordant sound of his own voice: the memory of the ants was still in it. He moved forward slowly, exasperated by the way his clumsy body refused to obey him and pushed his lower back impatiently from side to side instead of helping him go faster. He stopped again, one hand in the air, alert like a dog, brought up short by a new sensation which had been slow in coming because of his overexcitement: the lingering sensation in his raised hand of a cluster of tiny eggs and creatures with shells, which he had crushed. Again his limbs seemed locked, unable to move. His eyes were riveted on the patch of light, but his nerves were aware only of the crushed insects, only responded to their contact. Standing again now, he spat, looked down for a moment at the stones on the ground, the stones on which he could easily be crushed, and saw them swarming with insects. Danger made him forget his disgust, and he fell back onto the wall with the suddenness of a fleeing animal. He began moving forward again, his gummy hands sticking to the rotting leaves, numb with disgust, his whole being focused on that gap that was drawing him by the eyes. Like something exploding, it gave way to the sky. He stopped, bemused: from this position, he could no longer jump.

At last, he got to the corner of the wall and was able to climb down.

Flagstones overrun with low grass led to another dark mass, apparently a single tower: he knew how this kind of shrine was laid out. Free at last to run like a man, he threw himself forward, his head barely protected by his bent arm, risking cutting his throat open on a rattan liana.

No point in looking for carvings: the monument was un-finished.

2

The jungle had closed again over this abandoned hope. For days, the caravan had come across nothing but unimportant ruins: the Way of the Kings, both alive and dead, like a river bed, led to nothing but the vestiges left like bones by the migrations of tribes and armies. In the last village, men gathering wood had told them about a big building, the Ta Mean, located on the ridge of the hills between the Cambodian marches and an unexplored area of Siam, in a region inhabited by the Mois. 'Several hundred metres of bas-reliefs…'

If that was true, didn't a sinister, Tantalus-like torture await them? 'Impossible to take a single stone from the wall of Angkor Wat,' Perken had said. No doubt about that. Sweat ran down Claude's face and body, sticky and unbearable. Even though, in this jungle through which some wretched caravan of carts passed once a year, laden with glass jewellery that the natives would exchange for the savages' lacquer and cardamom, his life was surely worth the price of a bullet, he did not think the pirates would dare attack armed Europeans, unless they expected to make a big profit – these pirates, though, might know some temples – and yet anxiety hung over him. 'Was it fatigue?' he wondered; at that very moment, he realised that his eyes, which for a few minutes had been wandering over a mane of trees on a hill that had appeared through a gap, were following the smoke from a fire. For several days, they had not come across a single human being.

The natives had certainly seen the smoke. They were all following it with their eyes, their shoulders hunched as if confronted with a catastrophe. Despite the absence of wind, the smell of burnt flesh reached them. The animals came to a halt.

'Wild nomads…' Perken said. 'If they're burning their dead, they're all there…' He took out his revolver. 'But if they're holding the trail…'

He was already entering the foliage, with Claude at his heels. Their hands against their bodies for fear of the leeches which were already gathering on their clothes, their fingers tensed on their revolvers, they advanced, shoulders thrust forward, without a word. The foliage seemed suddenly transparent, making the jungle yellow, and Claude guessed there was a clearing: the opposite end of the jungle shone like water in the sun, dominated by thin palms above which the smoke continued to rise, vertical, heavy and slow. 'The most important thing is to stay inside the woods,' Perken said in a low voice. They were guided by muted noises. Claude was struck again by the smell of burning flesh. As soon as he could, he pushed aside the branches: above a row of bushes which stood in their way, a massive, chaotic movement of thick-lipped faces and spears with dazzling tips could be seen. The muted chanting lashed the foliage around them. The smoke was rising, thick and white, from a squat tower made of trelliswork in the middle of the clearing. At the top, four wooden buffalo heads, their horns as big as boats, stood out against the sky. Leaning on the shaft of his gleaming spear, scratching his head and bending towards the inside of the pyre, a yellow warrior watched, naked, his penis erect. Crouching, Claude was glued to this spectacle with his eyes, his hands, the leaves he could feel through his clothes, the panic that had seized him, as a child, whenever he saw snakes or live shellfish.

Perken was coming back. Claude stood up hurriedly, ready to shoot. As soon as the snapping of branches died out, the chanting could be heard again through the silence, weaker and weaker as they moved away from it...

They reached their caravan.

'Come on, let's get out of here!' Perken said, angrily.

The carts set off again quickly in an arpeggio of axles that resonated through every muscle in Claude's body. From time to time, the smoke appeared again, motionless, between the trees. As soon as they saw it, the natives tried to hurry their animals on, hunched over the shafts of the carts as if pursued by a holy terror. Now and then, large areas of orange-coloured rock appeared on the other side of a gully, and the tide of trees rose towards them, brilliant against a sky that was still a vivid blue. Every time a gap opened up in the jungle, they all stared at the distant treetops, fearing to see another fire: but nothing disturbed the motionless sky and the masses of foliage, above which the hot air shimmered in great vaporous waves, as if above a chimney.

Two more nights and two more days, and they came to a last village shivering with malaria, lost in the universal disintegration of things beneath the unseen sun. From time to time, they could see the mountains, ever closer. As the low branches fell back, they clattered and resonated on the roofs of the carts as on a soundbox; but this intermittent flagellation itself disintegrated in the heat. The only thing left to counter the stifling air that rose from the ground was the last guide's assertion that the monument towards which they were now walking was carved.

As always.

Although they doubted the existence of this temple, or any others that might be on their path, Claude still somehow trusted in them, with a perverse trust, made up of logical assertions and doubts so deep-seated they were almost physical, as if his eyes and nerves were protesting against his hopes, against the promises that had not been kept by this ghostly road.

At last, they reached a wall.

Claude's eyes were starting to become accustomed to the jungle. Near enough to make out the millipedes criss-crossing the stone, he saw that this guide, cleverer than the previous ones, had led them to a gap which could only mark the place where the entrance had once been. Like all the other temples, it was covered in tangled reeds. Perken, who by now knew everything about the vegetation around the monuments, pointed to a spot where the mass of reeds was less dense. 'The flagstones.' It was certain that they led to the shrine. The drivers set to work. The reeds, cut clean through, fell softly to right and left, with a noise like crumpled paper. The stalks lay on the ground, the pith looking very white in the gloom. 'If there are no carvings or statues in this temple,' Claude thought, 'what chance do we still have? No driver will go with Perken, the boy and me to the Ta Mean... Since we came across those savage tribes, all they want is to get out of here. And then how will only three of us manage to move the big bas-reliefs? The blocks weigh two tons... Statues might be possible. And we'll need a lot of luck... This is getting ridiculous, we're just like treasure hunters...'

He turned his eyes from the flashing machetes and looked back at the ground: the cut reeds were already turning brown. If he, too, had a machete, he could strike harder than these peasants! Oh, to cut like a scythe through the reeds! The guide touched him lightly to attract his attention: a last clump of reeds had fallen, and now, in the middle of the stones and the few reeds still standing, the blocks that formed the gate could be made out. They were smooth.

Once again, no carvings.

The guide was smiling, still pointing with his forefinger. Claude had never before felt such a strong desire to hit someone. Clenching his fists, he turned to Perken, who was also smiling. Claude's friendship for him changed all at once to rage, but he turned away in the direction of everyone else's eyes: the gate, which must once have been monumental, began in front of the wall and not where he had been searching for it. What all these men accustomed to the jungle were looking at was one of its corners, standing like a pyramid amid the debris: at the top, fragile but intact, a sandstone figure with a meticulously carved diadem. Peering between the leaves, Claude now made out a stone bird, with spread wings and a parrot's beak: a dense ray of sunlight fell on one of its feet. In this tiny, dazzling space, his anger vanished. He felt elated, grateful – to no one in particular – and then also curiously moved. He walked forward, heedless, possessed by the carving, until he was facing the gate. The lintel had collapsed, and with it everything that had surmounted it, but the twisted branches clutching the uprights, which had remained standing, formed a vault, both knotty and limp, through which no sunlight filtered. Fallen stones, their edges black against the light, barred the way into this tunnel, and beyond them stretched a curtain of pellitories, thin plants branching out into veins filled with sap. Perken punctured it, revealing the most extraordinary clutter, from which only a few triangular agave leaves emerged, with their mirror-like sheen. Claude went along the tunnel, from stone to stone, leaning on the walls, and wiped his hands on his trousers to rid them of the spongy sensation left by the moss. He suddenly remembered the wall with the ants: here, too, a bright gap, clogged with leaves, seemed to have dissolved into the murky light that had once again taken control of its decaying empire. Stones everywhere, some lying flat, almost all at an angle in the air: a building site invaded by the bush. Pieces of wall in purple sandstone, some carved, some bare, bracken hanging from them, a few with a red patina where they had been burnt. In front of him, bas-reliefs from the great era, very Indian in style – Claude went up to them – but very beautiful, surrounded old openings half-hidden beneath a rampart of fallen stones. He decided to look past them: above, reaching up to some two metres from the ground, three collapsed towers emerged from a mass of fallen stones so overwhelming that only dwarf vegetation could grow in it, as if it had been driven into the rubble. Yellow frogs were slowly moving away. The shadows had grown shorter: the invisible sun was climbing in the sky. Even though there was no wind, a motionless quivering, an endless vibration stirred the last leaves: the heat…

A loose stone fell, and echoed twice, dully at first then more clearly, making Claude think of the words: ve-ry stran-ge. More than these dead stones, lent a degree of animation by the progress of the frogs that had never seen men, more than this temple, so totally, overwhelmingly abandoned, more than the hidden violence of the plant life, it was something inhuman that caused an anguish to hang over the rubble and the voracious plants which clung to it like terrified animals, an anguish that protected, with the strength of a corpse, these figures whose centuries-old gestures held sway over a courtyard full of centipedes and other insects that lived in the ruins. Perken walked past him: this world, so like an underwater abyss, expired, like a jellyfish cast up on the seashore, suddenly powerless against two white men. 'I'm going to look for the tools.' His shadowy figure plunged into the tunnel from which the torn pellitories hung.

The main tower seemed to have collapsed entirely on one side: three of its walls were still standing, at the far end of the largest pile. Between them, a hole had at some point been dug deep in the ground: after the Siamese incendiaries, native treasure hunters had been here. In the very centre of the excavation, a pointed termites' nest rose, the colour of cement, almost certainly empty. Perken came back with a hacksaw and a stick in his hand, a hammer peeking out from his distended left pocket. He pulled out the head of a quarryman's sledgehammer and fixed it to the end of the stick.

'Svay has stayed in the village, as I told him.'

Claude had already seized the saw, whose nickel-plated mount glinted against the dark stone. Near one of the walls, which had collapsed sideways, its bas-relief within his reach, he hesitated.

'What's the matter?' Perken asked.

'It's absurd... I have a feeling this isn't going to work.'

He was seeing this stone as if for the first time; he could not shake off the feeling that the saw was unequal to the task, that what he was attempting was impossible. He made the block wet, and set to. The saw penetrated the sandstone, with a squeak. At the fifth attempt, he slipped it out of the notch: not a single tooth was left.

They had two dozen blades: the notch was one centimetre deep. He threw away the saw and looked in front of him: on the ground, a number of stones bore traces of bas-reliefs that had almost been erased. Obsessed as he had been by the walls, he had not paid them much attention. Could it be that the stones whose carved faces were turned towards the ground had been protected by the earth?

Perken had been thinking the same thing, and had called the drivers, who quickly made levers out of saplings and began turning the blocks over. The stone slowly rose, turned onto one of its sides, and fell back with a muffled sigh, revealing the traces of a figure behind the woodlice criss-crossing its surface in panic-stricken flight. Into the cavity left in the earth, as clean and polished as a mould, another block fell. One by one, the stones were showing their faces, eroded by the ground since the last century of the Siamese invasions, among the terrified insects whose quivering lines broke as they rushed towards the jungle in a minuscule frenzy. The more clearly the bas-reliefs showed their ravaged forms, the more certain Claude became that only the stones which formed one of the sections of the main temple that had remained standing could be removed.

Carved on both sides, the cornerstones represented two dancing girls: the motif was carved on three stones, one on top of the other. If they pushed the top one hard enough, it would be sure to fall.

'How much is it worth, in your opinion?' Perken asked.

'The two dancing girls?'

'Yes.'

'Hard to say. But certainly more than five hundred thousand francs.'

'Are you sure?'

'Yes.'

The machine guns he had been looking for in Europe: here they were, in this jungle he knew so well, in these stones… Were there temples like this in his territory? Perhaps he could get more out of them than his machine guns: if he found a few temples up there, couldn't he both arm his own men and intervene in Bangkok? Another temple: ten machine guns, two hundred rifles… Confronted with this monument, he forgot about the large number of temples without any carvings, he forgot about the Way… He imagined parades, the sun glinting on the barrels of the machine guns, the gleam of the sights…

Already Claude was having the ground cleared, to stop the stone from breaking when it hit another. While the men manoeuvred the blocks, he looked at the stone: one of the heads, its lips smiling in the manner of Khmer statues, was covered in very fine greyish-blue moss, like the down on a European peach. It took three men pushing it with their shoulders before it tipped over, fell on its edge and sunk in deep enough to stay upright. In being shifted, it had left two bright lines in the stone on which it had rested: colourless ants ran along these lines, busy saving their eggs. But this second stone, whose upper face now appeared, had not been placed there like the first; it was embedded in the still standing wall, held between two blocks of several tons each. To get it out would mean knocking down the whole wall, and if the stones of the carved sections, made out of carefully selected sandstone, were so difficult to handle, the others, which were enormous, would have to remain where they were for a few more centuries, or until the fig trees growing in the ruins cast them to the ground.

How had the Siamese managed to destroy so many temples? It was said they had used a large number of elephants, which they had attached to the walls… But there were no elephants now. It would therefore be necessary to cut or break this stone to separate the carved part, from which the last ants were fleeing, from the rough part embedded in the wall.

The drivers were waiting, leaning on their wooden levers. Perken had taken his hammer and a chisel from his pocket: clearly the most sensible thing to do was to chisel a narrow trench in the stone, and detach it like that. He set to work. But whether because he was using the tool badly, or because the sandstone was very hard, only a few fragments, a few millimetres thick, jumped out.

The natives would be even clumsier than he was.

Claude could not take his eyes off the stone: clear, solid and heavy against the quivering background of leaves and circles of sunlight, and charged with hostility. He could not make out the lines any more, or the sandstone dust: the last of the ants had gone, and every single one of their soft eggs with them. This stone was there, persistent, a living being, inert yet capable of refusal. A muffled, stupid anger rose in Claude: he braced himself and pushed the block with all his might. His exasperation was growing, searching for an object. Perken was watching him, his mouth half open, his hammer raised. This man who knew the jungle so well knew nothing about stones. Oh, to have been a mason for six months! What if they got all the men to pull together on a rope?… You might as well scratch it with your nails. And how to put a rope around it? His life was at stake here… His life. All the stubbornness, the concentrated will-power, the contained rage that had guided him through the jungle, were focused now on this barrier, this motionless stone that stood between him and Siam.

The more he looked at it, the more certain he was that he wouldn't reach the Ta Mean with his carts. And wouldn't the stones of the Ta Mean be similar to these? The will to conquer overwhelmed him like hunger or thirst, and he snatched the hammer from Perken and gripped the handle. In a rage, he attacked the stone with all his strength. The hammer rebounded several times, making a ridiculous noise in the silence: the polished nail extractor at the end of it shone as it passed through a ray of sunlight. He stopped, stared, then quickly, as if fearing his idea would get away, he turned the hammer round and struck again, very fast, close to the shiny notch left by Perken's chisel. A piece several centimetres in length flew out. Immediately, he let go of the hammer and rubbed his eyes… Fortunately, only the sandstone dust had got into them. As soon as he could see clearly again, he took his sunglasses out of his pocket and put them on to shield his eyes, then started hitting again. The nail extractor was an efficient tool, that obviated the need for a chisel: it reached the sandstone directly, with more force and much more frequently. With each blow, a wide flake flew off. In a few hours…

The natives would have to cut down the reeds blocking every path. Perken took the hammer again, and Claude moved aside with the drivers to clear the way. As he walked off, he heard the clear, rapid, unequal blows, like a message tapped out by a telegraph operator, louder than the noise of the scythed reeds, which sounded human and futile in the vast silence of the bush, in the heat… When he came back, flakes of sandstone littered the ground around a stream of dust. He was surprised by the colour of the dust: it was white, even though the sandstone was purple. Perken turned, and Claude saw the groove, as bright as the dust, and wide, since it was not always possible to strike in the same place…

He took over, while Perken continued supervising the clearing of the way to make a track for the blocks. It would be difficult to transport them: the simplest way would be to free them from the boulders around them and turn them so that they faced each other. Metre by metre, the trail grew longer beneath the shadows, which were vertical now. Only the sound of the hammer blows remained in this increasingly yellow light, these increasingly short shadows, this increasingly intense heat. The heat was not oppressive, but rather worked like a poison, relaxing the muscles little by little, draining them of strength along with the sweat that ran down their faces, mingled with the sandstone dust, and formed long rivulets under the sunglasses, like blood streaming from gouged eyes. Claude struck almost unconsciously, like a man lost in the desert. His thoughts were in shreds, shattered like the temple, alive now only with the excitement of counting the blows: one more, always one more… The jungle was disintegrating, the temple, everything… A prison wall, and these endless, endless hammer blows, like a file…

Suddenly, a void: everything came back to life, fell back into place as if everything around Claude had collapsed on top of him. He stood there motionless, aghast. Perken, aware that the noise had stopped, took a few steps back. The two sides of the nail extractor had broken.

He ran to Claude and took the hammer out of his hands, thinking he could somehow file the broken end into a new nail extractor, realised the absurdity of this idea, and struck the stone rapidly and furiously, just as Claude had done earlier. Finally he sat down, and forced himself to think. They had been prudent enough to bring several handles, but they only had one head…

Claude needed to shake off the sense of disaster that had overwhelmed him, to think clearly, as he had before he had thought of the nail extractor. The idea of using the hammer that way had come to him suddenly. Surely he could think of something else now? But he was overcome with fatigue, exhaustion, the disgust of a worn out creature. If only he could lie down… After so much effort, the jungle was again as powerful as a prison. He felt dependent, his will – his flesh itself – surrendered, as if, with each pulse, his blood was running out… He imagined himself sitting here, hugging his arms to his chest as if in a fever, hunched over, losing all consciousness, obeying the summons of the jungle and the heat with a feeling of liberation. And suddenly, terror gave him back the need to stand up for himself. The sandstone dust was running gently along the triangular gash, as shiny and white as salt, and falling like the sand in an hourglass, accentuating the mass of the stone, the stone which had again assumed its own life, as indestructible as a mountain: he could not take his eyes off it. He felt himself linked to it by hate as if to an animate being: it was watching over the route, watching over him, abruptly taking over the momentum that had been impelling him forward for months.

He made an effort to draw on his intelligence, which had been somehow diluted in this jungle… It was no longer a question of living with intelligence, but of living. Instinct, liberated by the numbing effect of the jungle, propelled him against this stone, his teeth clenched, his shoulder thrust forward.

Looking at the gash out of the corner of his eye as he would a watching beast, he took the quarryman's hammer, swivelled his whole body, and struck the block. The sandstone dust started flowing again. He looked at it, fascinated by the shining line. He concentrated his hate on it, and without taking his eyes off it, he struck a series of powerful blows, all the weight of his trunk and arms on the sledgehammer, swaying on his legs like a heavy pendulum. The only parts of his body that were still conscious were his arms and the small of his back: his life, the hopes of this past year, the sense of failure, everything came together in his anger and had no other existence except in the frenzied impact that shook his whole body, and liberated him from the jungle like a blaze of light.

He stopped. Perken had bent down by the corner of the wall.

'Look here: only the stone we're tackling is embedded. Look at the one underneath: it's simply been placed here, like the one on top was. We have to get it free first, then this one will be out of plumb, and since the gash has weakened it…'

Claude called two of the Cambodians and pulled with all his might on the stone underneath, while they pushed it. In vain: it was held by the earth, and most likely small plants too. He knew that Khmer temples had no foundations: he immediately had a small trench dug around it, then under it, to free it. The peasants, who had worked very quickly and very skilfully in digging around the stone, had slowed down now: they were afraid the block might crush their hands. He replaced them. When the hole was deep enough, he ordered a few trunks to be cut and had them placed as struts. The smell – stronger than ever – of the moist earth, the rotting leaves, the rain-washed stone, impregnated his soaked cotton clothes. At last, Perken and he were able to extract the stone: it toppled over, revealing its lower face covered with colourless woodlice which had sought refuge beneath it to escape the blows.

They now had the heads and feet of the dancing girls. The bodies alone remained on the second stone, which stood out from the wall like a horizontal crenel.

Perken picked up the sledgehammer and began again hitting the stone. He had hoped it would yield at the first blow, but this was not the case, and he continued striking, mechanically, once again overcome with rage… For a moment, he saw his parades without machine guns, overturned and laid waste as if trampled by wild elephants. The repeated blows, the loss of consciousness, gave him a kind of erotic pleasure, like any slow combat; these blows, again, bound him to the stone…

Suddenly – there was a different sound beneath the sledge-hammer – he held his breath. He tore off his glasses, and a blurred vision, blue and green, rushed in. But, while he blinked, another vision asserted itself, stronger than everything around him: the fracture! It sparkled in the sun, while the carved part, also bearing a clean cut, lay in the grass like a severed head.

He breathed at last, slowly, deeply. Claude, too, felt a sense of deliverance: if he had been weaker, he would have wept. The world was taking possession of him again, as if he were a drowned man coming back to life: the absurd gratitude he had felt when he had discovered the first carved figure once again overwhelmed him. Confronted with this fallen stone, and the fracture above, a sudden harmony was established between the jungle, the temple and himself. He imagined the three stones, placed one on top of the other: two dancing girls, among the purest he had ever seen. Now they had to be loaded on the carts. He could not take his mind off them: if he had been asleep, he would have woken up if anyone had tried to transport them. Now the natives were pushing the three blocks, one after the other, along the prepared track. He watched these things he had acquired with such difficulty, listening to the muffled thud as each of the sides, one by one, flattened the stalks of the reeds, and counting, half-consciously, the successive thuds, like a miser counting his money.

The natives stopped in front of the fallen stones of the gate. On the other side, the bullocks were not lowing, but could be heard scraping the earth with their hooves. Perken had two tree trunks cut down, tied ropes around one of the carved stones and fixed it to a trunk, which six natives tried to lift onto their shoulders. They could not manage it. Claude replaced two of them, one with the boy, the other with himself.

'Lift!'

This time the porters all stood up together, slowly, in total silence.

A branch snapped, followed by more branches, one after the other. The sound was getting closer. Claude had stopped, and was looking at the jungle but, once again, he could make out nothing. Someone from the last village, curious to see what they were doing, would not have hidden. Svay, perhaps? At a signal, Perken took Claude's place under the trunk. Claude took out his revolver and walked towards the place from which the noises had come. The natives, who had heard the snap of the holster being opened, then, like a weaker echo, the click as the safety catch was lifted, watched anxiously, uncomprehendingly. Perken, no longer able to support the trunk with his hands, took all its weight on his shoulder and also took out his revolver. Claude was beneath the trees now, but could see nothing but fairly dense shade, flecked here and there with spiders' webs. To try and find a native there, someone familiar with the jungle, was madness. Perken had not moved forward. Two metres above Claude's head, a number of branches were lowered then immediately sprang back again, releasing grey balls which dropped onto other branches, making them describe a large curve: monkeys. Furious and relieved at the same time, Claude turned, expecting to hear laughter. But none of the natives was laughing, and neither was Perken.

Claude walked towards him. 'Monkeys!'

'Not just monkeys: monkeys don't snap branches.'

Claude put his revolver back in its holster: a futile gesture in the silence which again descended on all these lives united in the stifling gangrene of the jungle…

He came back to the motionless group, and took his place again under the trunk. In a few minutes they had gone past the pile of fallen rocks. He had the carts brought as close as possible, so close that Perken had to order the drivers to move back in order to manoeuvre. Busy with the movements of the bullocks, they looked at the carved stones, bound by ropes, with complete indifference.

He was the last to go. The covered carts set off slowly beneath the foliage, bobbing unsteadily like boats on the sea. At each turn of the wheels, the shafts squeaked. At regular intervals, a muffled thud… Were the carts hitting a stump as they passed? He barely looked at the hole their passing had made in the greenery, the swaths of reeds on the ground, some, not completely crushed, slowly rising up again, the gap in the wall that gleamed every time it was struck by the ray of sunlight which had shone on the nail extractor. He felt his muscles relax: exhaustion was added to the heat, the drowsiness and the fever in him. The jungle, the lianas, the spongy leaves were losing their grip, though: these conquered stones were protecting him against them. His mind was no longer there: it was bound now to the onward movement of the loaded carts. They were moving away, creaking in a new way now because of their load, towards the nearby mountains. He shook some red ants off his sleeve, jumped on his horse, and joined the convoy. As soon as there was space to pass, he overtook the carts, one after the other: the drivers were still drowsy.

3

Night at last: another stage towards the mountains, the bullocks unharnessed from the carts, and, beneath the roof of the *sala* [1], as if in a pocket, the captive stones. It was as relaxing as a bath… Claude was walking between the piles that supported the straw huts. Protected by a little thatched roof, strips of wood were burning before rough clay Buddhas, pink points of light within the greater light of the moon. On the ground, a shadow overtook his feet, and silently approached his shadow. He turned. The boy stopped, black and distinct against the almost phosphorescent leaves of the banana trees.

'Mssié, Svay gone.'

'Are you sure?'

'Sure.'

'Good riddance.'

The barefoot boy disappeared, as if he had merged with the light that flooded the clearing. 'He's definitely not without his qualities,' Claude thought.

Obviously, Svay was following orders… Claude was not unhappy to be fighting a known enemy: in a specific conflict, he regained his determination. He lay down in the *sala*, where Perken was already asleep, lying on his stomach, his hands half-open.

He found it impossible to calm down, knowing that he had the stones. The voices of the peasants seemed to echo for a long time in the bright moonlight, then gradually became few and far between. The murmur of a storyteller and occasional raised voices still came from the village chief's hut. Then they, too, ceased, and the tropical silence descended, bound up with the moon-saturated air, disturbed from time to time by the solitary cry of a cockerel before that also vanished. The village was as quiet now as an extinct planet.

In the middle of the night, he was woken by a very weak, indistinct noise, so weak that he was surprised it had disturbed his sleep: a noise like foliage being dragged along the ground. His first thought was to check that the stones were still where he had placed them, between Perken's camp bed and his own. Pirates would not have chosen to attack a village while there were white men in it. He woke fully, his tiredness and laziness slipping away from him. He took a few steps outside the *sala*, but all he could see was the sleeping village and his own long blue shadow… He went back to bed, but remained on the alert for nearly an hour. Beneath the soft night wind, the air quivered like water. The only occasional sound was the increasingly infrequent bellow of bullocks roused briefly from their slumber… At last, he fell asleep again.

When he woke at sunrise, he felt such utter joy as he had rarely known. His determination, which had been impelling him towards such a doubtful course of action, for the last few months, had been justified. He jumped from the floor to the ground, without taking the ladder, and walked to the bucket of water. Near it, the boy was standing, striped from head to toe like a convict by the shadows of the branches.

'Mssié,' the boy said in a low voice, 'no way find carts in village.'

Instinctively on the defensive, Claude would have liked him to repeat what he had said, but immediately realised it would have been quite pointless. 'Where are they, carts from village?'

'Jungle, sure. Left in night.'

'Svay?'

'No one else know way to do that.'

Impossible to do the changeover, then. Without carts, no stones. That noise like boughs, last night…

'And our carts?'

'Drivers, sure not want go further. Me go ask?'

Claude ran to the *sala* and woke Perken, who smiled when he saw the stones.

'Svay ran away last night with the carts from the village and their drivers. So, no way we can change over. And the drivers we came with are going to want to go back to their own village, of course. Please wake up!'

Perken plunged his head in water. In the distance, monkeys cried. He dried himself and came back towards Claude, who was sitting on a bed, apparently counting on his fingers. 'First solution: go and find the fellows who ran away…'

'No.'

'A bucket of water certainly clears the head! Force our own drivers to carry on…'

'No. Take a hostage perhaps…'

'What do you mean?'

'Keep one of them prisoner and tell the others he'll be shot if they abandon us.'

Xa, his face like that of a serious, old-looking child, returned with two helmets in his hand: the sun was already high enough to reach their heads.

'Mssié; me go see. Our drivers gone too.'

'What?'

'Me say they not gone because me see carts. Our carts not gone, only village carts gone. But drivers all gone.'

Claude walked towards the straw hut behind which the carts had been left yesterday after they had returned from the temple: they were there, near where the small bullocks were tied. Had Svay been afraid that, if he came too close to the *sala* to get them, he would wake the white men?

'Xa, you know how to drive cart?'

'Sure, Mssié.'

The village was deserted, apart from a few women. Should they abandon the horses, and each drive a cart? It was only a matter of letting the bullocks follow the ones in front, driven by Xa. Three carts in all. It wasn't much. And to abandon the horses… If they were attacked, how could they defend themselves, with only carts? It took all the elation thrust on him by his will to continue, to keep moving forward, against the jungle and against men, to combat the sense of impoverishment caused by this desertion, which was beginning now, in the morning light, to give the jungle its power back.

'Xa,' Perken cried, 'where is guide?'

'He go away, Mssié…'

So now they had no guide. They would have to cross the mountains and find the pass alone, then, in the last villages, with their malaria-riddled natives, columns of mosquitoes whirling above their heads in the evening, as dense as rays of sunlight, to live, find drivers, keep moving on…

'We have the compass,' Claude said, 'and Xa. There are so few paths, they must be visible.'

'If you absolutely want to end up in a little heap swarming with insects, that seems a good way to go about it. Put your helmet on your head instead of keeping it in your hand, the sun's getting higher…'

'Let's try,' Claude would have liked to reply. But although he was anxious to get away from this village, whose inhabitants seemed to have fled before an invasion, from this clearing surrounded by great trunks which seemed even bigger in the morning light, he hesitated. He'd keep going, one way or another: that alone was certain. But how?

'In this region,' Perken went on, 'there are many men who know the way through the mountains. I'm going with Xa to Take, the little village without a *sala* that we saw before we got here. No chance of getting drivers. But I'll bring a guide: I don't think Svay has been that way.'

The boy was already getting the saddles ready.

The two figures, jolted by the trotting of the small horses, plunged into the trench of leaves, like miners into the earth. Although black, they appeared suddenly green from time to time, whenever a ray of sunlight beat down on the track… 'If they find a guide straight away,' Claude thought, 'and if they get him to run, they can be back by midday… Yes, *if they find a guide*…' But what if Svay had emptied Take as he had emptied this village?

The ladders had been taken inside the straw huts. Through the quivering air, everything began to move with an imperceptible, trancelike slowness, triggered by the coming of the great heat of day… He went and lay down on his camp bed, his chin in his hands. A guide to take them as far as the mountains? On either side of the clearing, around the circle of shimmering light and the man-made constructions, the jungle stretched, motionless and at the same time full of movement. On its surface, the light slowly shivered and broke up into a heat haze. It penetrated him, dulling his brain, each wave coming to die, warm and gentle, on his sweat-soaked skin, and he sank into a reverie dimmed by lengthy spells of sleep.

He was woken by the sound of horses' hooves, distant and hurried. Eleven o'clock… This guide was running extraordinarily fast. He frowned, and listened, without breathing. The noise rose from the earth: the horses were galloping, somewhere deep in the jungle… After running for two hours, a man couldn't follow galloping horses. Why were they in such a hurry? He tried hard to hear footsteps, but in vain: nothing but the great silence of the clearing, the soft hum of insects at ground level, and in the distance the staccato sound of the hooves…

He ran to the path. Clip-clop, clip-clop… The horses were getting closer. At last, he made out two shadows bobbing up and down. Then, as the two horsemen crossed a patch of sunlight, he saw them clearly, bent over the necks of the horses, their helmets pushed back: no one was running between them. He had the impression, not of a collapse, but of a slow, dull, irresistible disintegration… The two men, shadows once again, passed through another ray and were illumined again. Xa was more and more bent, and there were two white patches on his shoulders – hands – standing out against a vague shape: a man was riding pillion behind him.

'Well?'

Perken jumped off his horse. 'It's not looking good!'

'What about Svay?'

'He's doing his job well. He went over there and requisitioned those who know the passes to take them south.'

'But who's this fellow you've brought back?'

'He knows the way to the Moi villages.'

'Which are the tribes over there?'

'The Ke Diengs. They're part of the Stiengs. There's no other solution.'

'We have to go straight to rebel country?'

'Yes. If we follow the Way, we still have an unknown area, a controlled area and a rebel area. In the controlled area, God knows what the French authorities might dream up!'

'Ramèges is going to be furious when he finds out what we've got!'

'Which is why we absolutely have to forget about the big pass and go into rebel country. This guide knows how to get to the first Stieng village, where they barter. From there we can reach Siam across the smaller passes.'

'So we're heading west?'

'Yes.'

'And you don't know these Stiengs?'

'No, but obviously we have to choose the region where Grabot is. All the guide knows is that there's a white man over there. But he understands the Stieng dialect. In the village, we'll change guides – since we officially have to ask the chiefs for safe passage, we'll see what they say… I still have two Thermoses full of alcohol and the glass jewellery, that's more than enough to buy us safe passage… I don't know them, but I'm sure they know who I am. If Grabot doesn't want us to find him, he'll send a guide to make us take the long way round…'

'Are you sure they'll let us through?'

'We don't have any choice. In any case we have to go among the rebel tribes, sooner or later… The guide says these ones are warriors, but that they recognise the rice wine oath…'

The stocky Cambodian, his nose hooked like a Buddha, had left the horse and was waiting with folded hands. Somewhere, a machete was being sharpened on a stone, doubtless to open coconuts. Xa pricked up his ears. The noise stopped: through the holes in the trellises, the anxious women were observing the whites, their eyes darting here and there.

'Why did Grabot come here?'

'For sex, first of all – although the women in this region are much uglier than the ones in Laos. His definition of power has to include the possibility of abusing it…'

'Is he intelligent?'

Perken started laughing, but stopped immediately as if the sound of his own laughter had surprised him. 'When you know him, the question is comical, and yet… He's only ever thought about himself, or rather about what sets him apart, but the way other people think about gambling or power. He isn't someone, but he's certainly something. Because of his courage, he's much more separate from the world than you or me. He has no hopes, even half-formed ones. A liking for the things of the mind, however deteriorated, connects us to the universe. He told me one day, talking about "other people", about those for whom men like him don't exist, the "submissive" ones: "The only way to reach them is through their pleasure. We ought to invent something like syphilis." He arrived in the battalions full of enthusiasm towards the soldiers, though he didn't yet know them. On the boat, a canvas sheet separated the new ones from the repeat offenders and the recaptured fugitives. A canvas sheet with two or three holes. He starts to look through, but draws back abruptly: something happens, like a blow: a finger held out, with a nail half-chewed but still pointed, quite likely to scratch out his other eye… He's a man who's really *alone* – and like all men who are alone, he's obliged to fill his solitude, which he does with courage… I wish I could explain it to you…' He stopped to reflect.

'If all this is true,' Claude was thinking, 'he must have something indisputable to live on, something that allows him to admire himself…'

The rustle of insect wings strayed through the silence. A black pig walked slowly forward, as if it had taken possession of the silent village.

'This is more or less what he said to me: "If you get your face smashed in, you either give a damn or you don't. I'm playing a game of belote the others aren't playing because dying scares the pants off them. Not me: it'll be fine. And none too soon, given that it's just about the only thing I'm quite likely to do well. And ever since I stopped caring about dying, and in fact started quite liking the idea, I've been able to do whatever I want. If things go badly, they still can't go any further than my revolver… Easy enough to end it all…" And he really is very brave. He feels unintelligent and vulgar as soon as he's back in a city, so he compensates: to him, courage is a kind of family… In risking his life he finds the pleasure we all find, but with him it's keener because more necessary. And he's capable of going beyond risk. He's aiming for a kind of greatness, one that's elementary and with a strong dose of hatred, but out of the ordinary all the same: I told you how he lost his eye… To set off alone, absolutely alone, into that region, takes a lot of guts, too… Do you know the sting of the black scorpion? I'm familiar with the lash: the scorpion is more painful, and that's saying a lot. The first time he saw one, he felt a violent revulsion, so he went and got himself stung on purpose. To reject the world unconditionally means you're going to have to suffer terribly in order to prove your strength to yourself. In all that, there's an immense primitive pride, but life and quite a lot of suffering have finally given it a shape... Helping out a friend in some stupid business, he was almost eaten by ants – not as impressive as it seems at first sight, given his revolver theory.'

'So you don't think suicide is a solution?'

'It may not be any harder to die for yourself than to live for yourself, but I'm dubious... It's when you decline that you have to kill yourself, but it's when you decline that you start to love life again... But he believes it, that's the important thing.'

'What if he's dead?'

The straw huts were more closed than ever.

'They would have been selling European objects, and the guide would know it, because he goes to the barter village like everyone else. I questioned him: nothing has been sold. Officially, it's the village chiefs who we'll ask for safe passage anyway...' He looked around him. 'Women, nothing but women... A village of women... Doesn't that have any effect on you, this atmosphere with nothing masculine about it, all these women, this torpor... Doesn't it seem... fiercely sexual to you?'

'You can get excited when we've moved on. First, we have to get out of here.'

The boy gathered the baggage in one of the carts and attached the bullocks. The teams stopped, one after the other, in front of the *sala*, and the stones were lowered, with some difficulty, onto Claude's folding bed. At last the carts set off. The guide drove the first one, Xa the second. Claude, lying on the third, did not so much guide his bullocks as let them advance by themselves. Perken brought up the rear, on horseback. Claude's horse, which the boy had set free, followed slowly, head down. Perken was struck by its docility. 'It'd be wise not to abandon him,' he thought. And he tied it by its bridle to the last cart, ahead of him. Just as the village was about to disappear around the bend in the path, he turned: a few of the trellises had been lowered, and the women were watching, puzzled and curious.

Part Three

This rebel country, a half-savage place, was as uncertain and threatening as the jungle. In the barter village, which was even more decayed than the temples, the last terrified Cambodians evaded all questions about the villages, the chiefs, Grabot – although they seemed to have heard of Perken. This was a far cry from the voluptuous languor of Laos and Lower Cambodia: this was savagery, with its smell of meat. Finally, in exchange for two bottles of European alcohol, the messengers announced that they were being granted safe passage and would be provided with a guide. What they still did not know was who was granting this. But, ever since they had set out for Stieng territory, a graver anxiety had been hanging over them.

All at once, Perken stopped Claude, with a punch on the arm. 'Look at your feet, but don't move.'

Five centimetres from his right foot, two extremely sharp pieces of bamboo emerged, their tips like the tines of a fork.

Perken pointed.

'What now?'

He whistled between his teeth, without replying, and tossed his cigarette. It described an arc, very red in the greenish air made all the thicker by the declining daylight, and landed on the humus: beside it were two more of the sharp points.

'What are those things?'

'War spikes.'

Claude looked at the Moi, who was waiting for them, leaning on his crossbow: they had changed guides in the village. 'Couldn't that fellow have warned us?'

'This is bad…'

They resumed their march, dragging their heels on the ground, behind the guide, who was just a yellow patch now, only his dirty and bloodstained loincloth visible to Claude: he seemed neither completely animal, nor completely human. Every time he was forced to lift his foot instead of scraping it on the ground – because of stumps or trunks – the muscles of his leg contracted, with the fear of walking too fast. This connected Claude to the danger and he moved forward like a blind man. No matter how hard he tried, his eyes were almost useless here, and he had to rely on his sense of smell. The gusts of hot air that assaulted his nostrils were full of the smell of humus, which jarred his nerves: how was it possible to see the spikes when the path was covered with rotting leaves? He felt as dependent as a slave with his legs tied… He struggled against this cautious pace, but his taut calves were stronger than his mind.

'What about our bullocks, Perken? If one of them falls…'

'No risk of that: they can sense the spikes better than we can.'

Should they climb into the carts, which were behind them, led only by Xa? That would make it harder to defend themselves in case of attack…

They crossed a dried-up river bed, as restful as a halt, with its stones that could hide nothing. A few metres away, three Mois stood on the clay embankment, one above the other, watching them. There was something inhuman about their stillness, as if it came not from them but from the silence.

'If things turn nasty, we'll have enemies behind us, too.'

The three savages followed them with their eyes, still motionless: only one carried a crossbow. The path was less dark now, the trees sparser: it was still necessary to walk carefully, but the obsession was fading. At last, the light of a clearing appeared at the end of the path.

The guide came to a halt in front of some thin rattan lianas stretched at neck height, and pulled them off. Their little thorns glinted in the sunlight and were swallowed by it. Claude had not even seen them. 'If things go badly,' he thought, 'it won't be easy getting out of here in a hurry.'

The Moi carefully replaced the lianas.

There was no path across the clearing. The one they had been on led into it and continued beyond it. Calm as it was, this clearing, where they were going to have to sleep, felt like a trap: one half shrouded in shadow, the other glowing with the very yellow light that preceded nightfall. No palms: Asia was present only in the heat, the colossal dimensions of some of the red trees and the dense silence, made all the more solemn and expansive by the rustling of the myriads of insects and the occasional solitary cry of a bird swooping down onto one of the highest branches. The silence closed over these lost cries like stagnant water; up above, a branch swayed slowly, almost drowned in the chaos of the evening, while beyond all this vegetation devoid of paths or tracks, its depths shrouded in mist, the mountains stood out against the already lifeless sky. Like shipworms in the giant trees, the Mois used small, deadly weapons. In this isolated place, their subterranean existence and their inexplicable caution seemed all the more threatening. For three men without an escort, led by a guide they had been freely given, there was no need for spikes and rattan lianas. Why protect the clearing in that way? 'Is Grabot determined to ensure his freedom at all costs?' Claude thought; and as if thought was so rare in this place that it was instantly communicated, Perken guessed his question:

'I'm convinced he's not the only one...'

'Meaning what?'

'Not the only chief. Or else, he's gone completely native...' He hesitated. The words seemed to spread through the sombre vegetation, and were vindicated almost immediately by the crouching guide, who was scratching the white patch of a skin disease on his knee. '...and has changed utterly...'

The unknown again. The man was as much a constant of this expedition as the invisible line of the Way of the Kings. He, too, was keeping them from their destiny. Yet he had granted them safe passage…

The photos Perken had brought from Bangkok haunted Claude: a jolly, strapping one-eyed fellow, his helmet tipped back on his head, whether in the bush or in the Chinese bars of Siam, laughing heartily, with his mouth open and his eyebrows raised. He was familiar with faces like that, in which the child's expression can be glimpsed beneath the man's boorishness, in laughter, in eyes wide with surprise, in gestures: helmet pushed down with a big slap over a friend's ears, or a foe's… What was left in this place of the city man? 'Unless he's gone completely native…'

Claude searched for the guide: he was chanting, with Xa as an audience, near the motionless bullocks. The fires had been lit for the night, and were crackling softly, not far from the beds, which had been unfolded and covered with mosquito nets: no tents because of the heat.

'Take the mosquito nets off,' Perken said. 'It's bad enough that we're fully lit because of this damned fire. Let's at least try to see anyone attacking us!'

The clearing was vast, and any attackers would first have to come over open ground.

'If something happens, the one who's watching shoots the guide, and we run behind this bush on the right, to get out of the light…'

'Even if we come out the winners, without a guide…'

All the things hanging over them seemed to be in Grabot's hands, as if he had them under lock and key.

'What do you think he'll do, Perken?'

'Grabot?'

'Of course!'

'We're close to him, we expect a lot from him, but I really don't know what to predict…'

The fire was still crackling, but the flame rose straight and bright, almost pink, lighting only the spasmodic curls of its own smoke, casting reflections on the massed foliage, which by now was barely distinguishable from the sky. He was staking everything on the man, but he did not know him.

'Despite the spikes,' Claude said, 'do you think he's going to let us through?'

'If he's alone, yes.'

'And are you sure he doesn't know how valuable these stones are?'

Perken shrugged. 'He's uneducated. Just like me…'

'And if he's not alone, who's with him?'

'Certainly not a white man. And loyalty means a lot to anyone who dares to come up here. I've done Grabot favours in the past…' He looked down at the grass, reflectively. 'I'd like to know what he's defending himself against… Your old dreams, your own decay, are what stoke your passions…'

'We still don't know what his passions are.'

'I told you about a man who had himself tied up naked by women in Bangkok… That was him. It's not that much more absurd than claiming to sleep and live – live! – with another human being… But he's terribly humiliated by it…'

'By the fact that it's known about?'

'No one knows about it. The fact that he did it. So *he compensates*. I'm sure that's the main reason he's come here… Courage compensates… To escape the burden of shame, even a small one, all you need is this…'

As if human gestures were too narrow to encompass this vastness, he used his chin to indicate the clearing and the hills receding into the shadows. From the wall of trees to the distant vistas merging into the darkness, from the sky, in which the stars seemed brighter than the fire, to the great primeval jungle, the slow, massive force of the coming of night overwhelmed

Claude with a sense of solitude, made him feel once again that he was being pursued. It engulfed him, like an overpowering sense of indifference, like the certainty of death.

'I can well understand that he doesn't give a damn about death...'

'It isn't death he's not afraid of, it's being killed: he doesn't know anything about death. Not to be afraid of getting a bullet in the head is nothing special.' He lowered his voice. 'In the stomach, now that's quite a bit worse... That lasts... You know as well as I do that life has no meaning: even if you live alone, you can't really escape worrying about your fate... Death is always there, you understand, as... as irrefutable evidence of the absurdity of life...'

'For everyone.'

'For no one! No one really believes in it. Not many people could live... All they think about is the fact that – oh, how can I make you understand? – that they could be killed, that's it. And that's of no importance. Death is something else: it's the opposite. You're too young. I didn't understand it until I saw a woman grow old... yes, a woman... I told you about Sarah, didn't I?... Then, as if that warning wasn't enough, when I found myself impotent for the first time...'

The words were torn from him, only reaching the surface after breaking through a thousand clinging roots.

'*Never in front of a dead man...*' he went on. 'Growing old, that's it, growing old. Especially when you're separate from other people. Decay. The thing that weighs heavy on me is – how can I put it? – my condition as a man: the fact that I'm growing old, that this horrible thing called time is growing inside me, inexorably, like a cancer... Time, there you are... All these damned insects buzzing around our lamp are slaves to the light. These termites in their hives are slaves to their hives. I don't want to be a slave to anything.'

The jungle had found a close correlation in the vast onward movement of the night: the savage life of the earth rose with the darkness. Claude could ask no more questions: the words that formed in his mind passed over Perken as if he were an underground river. Separated, by the whole jungle, from those for whom reason and truth existed, was the man opposite him looking for human assistance against his ghosts crowding around him in the darkness? He had taken out his revolver: the barrel glinted weakly in the shadows.

'My whole life depends on what I think of the gesture of putting this barrel in my mouth and pressing the trigger. Do I think "I'm destroying myself" or do I think "I'm doing something positive"? Life is a substance, you have to know what to do with it – not that we ever do anything with it, but there are several ways of not doing anything... To live *in a certain way*, you have to put an end to the things that threaten you, decay and all the rest: then a revolver is a good standby: it's easy to kill yourself when death is a means to an end... That's where Grabot's strength lies...'

Total darkness had fallen at last, spreading to the furthest recesses of Asia. Night and silence established their dominion once again over the vast emptiness. Above the low sound of the fires, the voices of the two natives rose, clear and monotonous, but without carrying, trapped. Very close to them, a sturdy alarm clock beat its precise measure against the endless silence of the bush. More than the fires, more than the voices, it was this ticking that connected Claude to the life of men, through its constancy, its clarity, the invincibility shared by all mechanical objects. His thoughts emerged, but nourished by the depths from which they had escaped, and still dominated by the power of the supernatural that rose from the night and the burnt earth, as if everything, even the earth, had undertaken to convince him of the wretchedness of mankind.

'And the *other* death, the death which is inside us?'

'To exist against all that' – Perken looked around at the threatening majesty of the night – 'do you understand what that means? To exist against death is the same thing. It seems to me sometimes that I'm risking everything on that hour. And perhaps everything will be settled soon, with some more or less filthy arrow…'

'We don't choose our own death…'

'But accepting that I can't choose my death has made me choose life.'

The reflection of the fire on his shoulder moved: he must have reached out his hand. It was a small gesture, just as he himself seemed small and human, with his feet lost in the shadows and his staccato voice in the star-filled vastness. Only that voice, between the dazzling sky on the one hand and death and the underworld on the other, came from a man, but there was something so inhuman in it that Claude felt as separate from it as he would from the beginnings of madness.

'You want to die with an intense awareness of death, without… weakening?'

'I almost died. You can't imagine the joy that comes when you're confronted with the absurdity of life, like being confronted by a woman who's…' – he made a tearing gesture – '…suddenly stripped naked.'

Claude found it hard to take his eyes away from the stars. 'We almost all make a mess of our deaths…'

'I spend my life seeing mine. And what you're trying to say – because you're afraid, too – is true: it may be that it's stronger than me. Too bad! There's also something… satisfying in life being stamped out…'

'You're never really thought of killing yourself?'

'I don't think about my death in order to die, but in order to live.'

The intensity in his voice was not like that of any other passion: it was a poignant, hopeless joy, like a piece of wreckage rescued from an abyss as deep as that of the darkness around them.

2

Since waking, they had walked for hours, between the spikes – less numerous now – and the leeches. From time to time, the loud cries of the monkeys reverberated to the far end of the valley, interrupted by the muffled thud of the cartwheels against the stumps.

They could see the Stieng village now, at the end of the path, as if through the clouded lens of a pair of binoculars. It had overrun the clearing. To Claude, its wooden ramparts looked like a strange weapon. Those beams erected into a barrier, concealing the jungle – they were quite close now – bore violent witness to a force, evoked, to the point of anguish, a feeling accentuated by the only objects emerging above the rampart: a grave decorated with fetishes made out of feathers, and a huge *gaur*[2] skull. The horns shimmered in the heat haze, as if the jungle, which had vanished behind the high barricade, had left nothing in its place but these strange objects embedded in a sky free of leaves. The guide again moved aside a few rattan lianas and put them back in place again after the carts had passed.

They entered through the half-open gate. The Moi who was guarding it closed it behind them with the barrel of his rifle: 'At last something from Grabot!' Claude said. 'He hasn't lowered the lever on his rifle,' Perken thought: but the wooden sound of the gate closing impelled him forward.

To the right, squat huts arranged almost at random, half-buried in the ground like beasts of the jungle, small dogs left to fend for themselves, yapping on a heap of rubbish, men and women watching intently over the tops of the trellises.

The guide led them towards a hut that was taller than the others, raised in the middle of an open space next to the pole that supported the *gaur*: it dominated this peopled solitude, as did the huge horns pointing up into the sky like raised arms. A communal house or a chief's house: perhaps Grabot was here, beneath this palm roof, beneath these horns… They were still alive, which meant he had protected them so far. Following the guide, they climbed the ladder, entered and crouched.

They could not yet make out anything, but they sensed that there was no white man here. Perken stood up, took a few steps, and crouched again, a quarter turned, as if in deference. Claude imitated him. In front of them now – they had previously been behind them – at the far end of the hut, about ten warriors were standing, armed with the short weapon of the Stiengs, half sabre, half machete. One of them was scratching himself: Perken had heard the rustle of his nails before seeing him.

'Free your safety catch,' he said very quickly, in a low voice.

He couldn't mean the Colt that Claude carried in his belt. He heard a very slight click, and saw Perken pull some of the glass jewels from his pocket. He immediately lifted the catch of his little Browning deep inside his own pocket – slowly, so as not to be heard – and took out some blue pearls. Perken held out his hand, and passed them on, together with his jewels, saying some phrases in Siamese which the guide translated.

'Look, Claude, above the old man I think is the chief.'

A clear patch in the shadows: a white European jacket. 'Grabot must be here.' The old chief was smiling, his lips stretched over his gums: he raised two fingers. 'They're going to bring the jar,'[3] Perken said.

A triangle of sunlight entered the hut, cutting the old man in two from the shoulder to the hip, leaving his eunuch-like head in darkness, and emphasising his collarbones and ribs. He looked from the white men to the shadow of the skull projected in front of him, as distinct as a paper cut-out, even though perspective made the two horns appear as one. There was a sudden thud, as if something had been knocked against, and the shadow quivered. A jar appeared above the ladder, a bamboo reed in its neck, two hands with elongated fingers placed respectfully on either side, like handles. With those two vertical wrists to support it, it seemed as if the jar was being offered to the still quivering shadow, in appeasement. More slight thuds: the jar carrier, who must have knocked against the pole in passing, was trying to find the rungs of the ladder. He finally appeared, slow and upright, above floor level, covered in the blue rags of the Cambodians – even the Moi chief was clad only in a loincloth – and lowered the jar, with mysterious caution, to the floor in front of him. Xa's hand tightened on Claude's knee.

'What's got into you?'

The boy asked the Cambodian with the jar a question. He turned to him, and then immediately, violently, towards the chief.

The boy dug his nails into Claude's flesh. 'He… he…'

Claude suddenly realised that the man was blind. But there was something else.

'Kmer Mieng!' Xa cried to Perken.

'Cambodian slave.'

The man sank down again towards the village, cut off by the floor of the hut: Claude waited for another thud, as if he were required to knock against the perch again on his way. But the anxious expectation of the men, the very silence, seemed to hang over the chief's hand, which he had raised solemnly over the jar. He lowered it and sucked the alcohol through the bamboo reed, his eyes closed. He passed the pipe to Claude, who took it without any revulsion: his anxiety was too strong, an anxiety made all the stronger by the way Perken's eyes kept darting outside, trying to see what was happening there.

'I'm really worried by the fact that Grabot isn't here. We're making a commitment to the Mois, and he isn't. I trust him, but all the same…'

'But are they… making a commitment… or not?'

'None of them would dare betray the rice wine. But if he hasn't made a commitment to them, then God alone knows…'

He said something in Siamese, and the guide translated. The chief replied with a single sentence.

This reply aroused unusual interest in the men at the back, although they remained motionless, except when they scratched themselves. Claude finally made them out, his eye drawn to the white patches of skin disease on their bodies. All of them were now watching attentively.

'He says there's no white chief,' Perken translated. He looked again at the jacket. 'I'm sure he's here!'

Claude remembered the rifle, and also looked at the jacket. It seemed to have two shadows, its own and the dust. 'The jacket hasn't been worn for a long time,' he said, in a low voice, as if afraid they would understand him.

Perhaps the dust accumulated very quickly here. The floor, though, was clean, and so were the fetish candle holders. It was highly unlikely that Grabot would dress the same way here as he dressed in Bangkok, but the words Perken had spoken in the clearing came back to Claude, as if they had been hanging in this hut for several minutes: 'Unless he's gone completely native…' Why was he hiding, letting these men, with their eyes as intent as the eyes of animals, stand in for him?

Perken was again talking to the chief. The conversation was very short.

'He says he agrees, which means absolutely nothing. Frankly, I'm suspicious… To be on the safe side, I said we'd come back this way, and bring him some gongs and jars, in addition to the Thermoses of alcohol I'd been intending to give him. Then he'd have more reason to murder us on the way back... He doesn't believe me... There's something not quite right here. We really must get hold of Grabot! If we confronted him, he wouldn't dare...'

He stood up: the parleying was over. He went to the ladder, walking around the shadow of the skull as if fearing to come into contact with it. The guide led them to an empty hut. The village was gradually coming back to life: the trellises were lowered, and men in loincloths or in blue rags – the slaves – bustled around the hut they had just left, with the restrained excitement of blind men. Perken kept walking, but without taking his eyes off them. One of them was starting to cross the empty space they themselves had entered: their paths might meet. Perken stopped, took his foot in his hand as if he had stepped on a thorn, and looked at it closely, leaning on Xa to keep his balance.

'When we meet up with that one, ask him which is the white man's hut. Which is the white man's hut. Nothing else. Understand?'

The boy did not reply. The slave had almost reached them: no time to explain again. He was within reach of their voices... Had they missed him? No: almost chest to chest with him, the boy was saying something. The other man looked down at the ground and replied, also in a low voice. 'Does he think he's answering another slave?' Perken tried to go closer to Xa, to touch him, get him to translate quickly, and almost fell headlong: he had forgotten he was still holding his foot. The boy had seen Perken's clumsy move, and although he had moved a few steps away, he held out his arms. Perken grabbed hold of his wrist. 'Well?' Xa was looking at him with the worried and resigned look of a native accustomed to the follies of white men, surprised by his abruptness and the way he lowered his voice as though someone could hear and understand them, here on this clearing of beaten earth that was empty now except for the slave, who had resumed walking, and a dog running towards the shade.

'Near the banana trees.'

The words were unambiguous: there was only one clump of half-wild banana trees in the clearing. Next to them, a big hut. Claude turned, intrigued, vaguely guessing what was happening.

'The slave says he's in that hut.'

'Grabot? Which hut?'

Cautiously, Perken pointed to it, his hand on his hip.

'Shall we go?'

'Let's untie our bullocks first. Then it'll look as if we came across it by chance… well, as much by chance as possible…'

They rejoined the guide. In front of the hut that had been assigned to them, Xa began to unharness the bullocks.

'That's enough,' Perken said. 'Now let's go!'

'If you want.'

Although they were approaching it in a roundabout way, the hut by the banana trees exerted a strong pull on them. Whether they wasted time in discussions or not, they were at Grabot's mercy. If they had to come to an understanding, the sooner the better.

'What if things turn nasty?' Claude asked.

'I shoot him. It's our only chance. In the jungle, in his territory, we're done for…'

Grabot was surely familiar with the kind of revolvers that could be fired through trousers… They had arrived. A windowless hut, its opening covered, not with a trellis, but a rudimentary door. The latch had been closed *on the outside*. 'There has to be another entrance.' A dog began howling behind the hut.

'If he carries on like that,' Perken thought, 'they'll all come running.' He pushed the latch and pulled the door to him, hesitantly, fearing that it was also locked on the inside. It gave, with a slowness that matched his anxiety, because the wood had changed size during the rainy season.

A small bell was ringing. A shaft of sunlight fell slantwise from the roof, dense with dark blue specks. Shadowy forms were turning as if around an axle, rising and falling as they went. The highest of them became more distinct as it came into view from the side: a horizontal crosspiece. There was something at the end, pulling it. It was revolving around what looked like a big tub or vat… It was turning in their direction, losing its shape as it moved away from the dazzling shaft of sunlight. On the dusty ground, where the light hit, their shadows were intertwined, with long trunks and short legs. At last the whole contraption appeared in the rectangle of light falling through the door: a millstone. The ringing stopped.

Perken had moved back into the shade to see better, and Claude followed him sideways, like a crab, incapable either of staying where he was or of turning his eyes away and walking out of the light that penetrated the hut like a block of stone. But Perken was still retreating. A terrified retreat: Claude could make out his fingers tensing as if to grip something, his astonished stagger. Now he stopped, and stood there in silence. There was a slave attached to the millstone. A slave with a beard. A white man?

Outside, a dog howled. Perken shouted something, so quickly that Claude did not understand. He began again, breathless. 'What happened?'

The slave thrust himself forward, in the darkness, his shoulders trembling. The little bell rang again, just once. But the man stopped.

'Grabot?' Perken yelled.

The horror and the questioning in his voice beat against the face that was turned towards them. Claude searched for the eyes, but could make out only the beard and the nose. The man held out his open hand, the fingers outstretched, as if trying to take something, then let it fall again against his thigh with a slap. He was attached with leather straps. 'Is he blind?' Claude wondered, incapable of uttering the word, of questioning Perken.

But the man's dirt-stained face was turned towards them. Towards them, or towards the light? Claude could not see his eyes, but Perken had said that Grabot was one-eyed, and the man's body was three quarters turned towards the door.

'Grabot!' Perken cried, hoping he would not reply, and at the same time…

The man said a few words, in a voice that sounded false.

'*Was*?' Perken cried, almost choking.

'He didn't speak German!'

'No, he spoke Moi: I was the one who… What? What?'

The slave tried to advance towards them, but he was held by the straps to the end of the crosspiece, and each time he moved he was pushed back into the orbit of the millstone, either to the right or to the left.

'Turn round, for God's sake!'

Immediately, the two white men realised that what they dreaded most was the thought of this creature coming anywhere near them. Neither revulsion, nor fear: a holy terror, a horror of the inhuman, such as Claude had known earlier when confronted with the pyre. The man again took two steps forward. The bell rang again, and he stopped.

'But he's understood,' Claude murmured.

He had understood that sentence, too, even though Claude spoken in a very low voice. 'What are you?' he said at last in French, in his toneless voice.

A kind of despair took hold of Claude, as if he were mute. The question could mean so many things. What to reply: Frenchmen, white men, or what?

'The bastards!' Perken stammered. The questioning tone in which he had spoken until then, even in the command to turn round, had vanished. His voice now was filled with hate. He approached and said his name. Now Claude could quite clearly see the man's two eyelids, stretched over his absent eyes. How to touch him, how to finally establish some kind of connection with him? How to get anything coherent from that obliterated face, beneath those eyelids with their vertical furrows, beneath that terrible filth? Perken's hands gripped the man's shoulders. 'What? What?'

Even though Perken was so close to him, the man had turned his head, not to Perken, but to the light. His cheeks tensed: he was finally going to speak. Claude waited for the voice, terrified by what he expected from it. At last it came:

'Nothing…'

The man was not mad. He had dragged out the word, as if he was still searching. But this was not a man who could not remember, or who did not want to reply: it was a man who was saying *his truth*. And yet – Claude could not forget: 'Easy enough to end it all' – he was a dead man. They would have to revive a corpse, like massaging a drowned man…

The door slammed shut, and they were cast back into a dungeon-like gloom. Claude looked up questioningly: the Mois – the same Mois – were there, around him. Feeling imprisoned by the darkness, he rushed to the door, pulled it open quickly, and turned. Just as when they had first come in, the man, struck by the daylight, took one step forward with his little bell, shaking like a terrified animal: it was a reflex reaction to the light and the voice combined. Perken picked up the stick which had fallen into the rectangle of light after Claude's move: it was a throatlash, a branch with a bamboo tip like the spikes. He wanted to take a look at the man's shoulders, but his back was turned away from them. He took out his knife and started cutting the straps: it was difficult to get the blade through the rough but skilful knots, and he had to cut as far as he could from the arms. He was obliged to go closer, and cut the line. The other man was free now, but did not move.

'You can come forward!'

He started moving along the wall, following his old route, pulling with his lower back, and almost fell. Without knowing why, Perken turned him slightly, and pushed him towards the door. He stopped again, aware suddenly of the freedom in his shoulders. He immediately stretched out his hand: the first gesture to indicate clearly that he was blind. Perken put his hand, which felt unused since he had finished cutting, back on the crossbeam. There, it touched the damned bell. He cut it off and flung it through the door. It rang as it hit the ground, and the man opened his mouth, no doubt in astonishment. Perken looked in the direction of the sound: a few metres outside, some of the Mois were trying to see into the hut. There were lots of them: several rows of heads above bowed bodies.

'Let's get out of here before anything else!' Claude said.

'Take the first steps with your eyes closed! Otherwise, you'll hesitate when you get out in the sun and they're quite capable of attacking you.'

He had the feeling that, if he closed his eyes at that moment, he would never open them again. He thrust himself forward, looking down at the ground, concentrating all his strength on not stopping. The line of Mois drew back: only one remained. 'The slave's master,' Perken thought. He walked up to him. '*Phya*,' he said.

The Moi swung his shoulders, then moved aside.

'What did you say?'

'*Phya* – chief. That's the word the interpreter kept using. Perhaps it's just putting off the inevitable… But where's the other one, damn it?'

The blind man had not followed them: he was in the doorway of the hut, looking even more fearsome in daylight. Perken walked back and took him by the arm.

'To our hut.'

The Mois were following them.

3

The chief's hut was empty. On the wall, in the shadows, the white jacket. The Mois stood around them in a semicircle, a little distance from them. Perken recognised the guide.

'Where's the chief?'

The Moi hesitated, as if hostilities had already broken out. But then he made up his mind. 'Gone. Come back tonight.'

'Is he lying?' Claude asked Perken.

'Let's get to our hut first, as quick as we can!'

Each of them took Grabot beneath one arm.

'No, I don't think he's lying: my questions about the white chief disturbed him… At a time like this, the only reason he could have left was to ask the neighbouring villages for help if things turn nasty.'

'In other words, it's a trap.'

'Things are getting complicated without our help…'

They were talking to each other across Grabot's lifeless profile.

'Wouldn't it be more sensible to leave before he returns?'

'The jungle is a bigger danger than they are…'

Leaving immediately would mean abandoning the provisions and the stones… Without a guide, they'd be heading for certain death.

They had reached their hut.

Xa looked at them with an expression of horror on his face, but almost no surprise.

'Shall we harness the bullocks?' Claude asked.

Perken looked at the top of the wooden rampart, and shrugged. 'They're gathering...'

The Mois had stopped following them. Others were already joining them, and they were armed. And once again, as if nothing could overcome the forms of the hidden jungle, Claude was back in the world of insects: from the scattered huts, silent and apparently newly abandoned, the Mois were emerging, although he could not see through where, and streaming onto the path with precise movements like wasps, their weapons like mantises. Crossbows and spears occasionally stood out against the sky, as clearly as antennae. The men kept arriving. They did not cry out, made no sound other than the scuffling of their feet in the bushes. The bellowing of a black pig filled the clearing and faded. The silence melted once more into the sunlight, and the constant arrival of the men again dominated the clearing.

The white men and Xa were back in their hut, having fetched their guns and cartridges. They could still see the carts, a stone peeping out above them. How could they defend themselves in a hut raised on piles, closed on three sides, open in front of them? A trellis lay on the ground. They immediately lifted it and placed it across the opening: it was one metre high, and would only protect the top halves of their bodies. When the arrows started flying, they would have to lie down. It was like being inside a fairground booth; through the rectangle of the opening, beyond the deserted clearing, the Mois came and went from one section of the rampart to another, between the huts and the cultivated trees. In front of them, the empty clearing struggled against the enemy silence.

'Listen, Grabot, you know them. We're in the hut to the right of the chief's hut. Apparently they're starting to move. What are they going to do?… Answer, for God's sake! Do you understand?'

Silence. A mosquito hummed in Perken's ear. He slapped himself in irritation.

At last, the voice: 'What bloody difference does it make?'

'Do you want to stay here?'

He shook his head, absurdly. But there was no negation in his eyes, which made the movement of the neck seem animalistic, like the movement of a bull, like the expression in his almost inhuman voice. 'What bloody difference does it make now?'

'Now that you're…'

'Now that I'm what?'

'It can be sorted out…'

'And what about their bloody dogs, who were given my eye to eat – will you sort them out, too?'

Lines with pointed tips appeared through the opening: more spears, on the other side of the clearing.

'Who's with us in this hut? There's you, this other one who I guess is a young fellow, and who else?'

'The boy.'

'Is that all? And they're all around?'

'All I can see is the clearing.' With his knife, he made two narrow holes in the wall. 'There aren't any on the other sides.'

'They'll come… At night all they have to do is start a fire under us… That's almost the way it happened to me… As if it made any difference!'

Silence. The cross-hatched spears had vanished: the warriors were crouching now…

'How do we get out of this?' Claude wondered.

'Are you planning on dying here?' He was shaking his fists, even though Grabot could not see them – imprisoned this time in his universe of forms just as Grabot was in his walled-in head. How to convince a blind man? He closed his own eyes, tightly, searching for other words.

But Grabot opened his mouth. 'If you shoot one, tie him up and pass him to me...'

Claude had been looking at a spear that had reappeared, but the last words were so striking that he looked away from it. They were harsh words, emerging from an abyss of humiliation, but not bestial: what made them horrible was their simplicity. In the other hut, they had tried in vain to arouse the man's spirit: had it now returned only to reveal the most horrifying degeneration? And those dreams of torture, those tensed fingers, whose eyes were those nails ready to gouge? The hand was shaking at the end of the arm: there was no expression on the face, but the toes were curled. This body could speak – as soon as they had opened the hut with the millstone, that hand held out for food, that back accustomed to the throatlash – and only of what it had suffered. It spoke so eloquently that Claude forgot, for a moment, that they themselves were the ones most likely to be tortured. They could do nothing against fire. Nothing. The cry of a peacock rose, and vanished in the intense calm of the sky. The crouching Mois might have been drowsing were it not for their intent hunters' eyes. Over all those faces, the air was stretched to breaking point, like a kestrel hovering motionless in the sky. For as long as the daylight lasted.

'Do you think they'll start a fire, Perken?'

'No doubt about it.'

Grabot had fallen silent.

'They're waiting for something: either the arrival of the chief, or nightfall. Or both... You can be sure they're feeling confident.'

Because of the tone, Claude thought at first that Perken had been speaking to Grabot.

'So wouldn't it be better to open fire and try to reach the gate? We have plenty of cartridges… I know it's a chance in a hundred… But maybe they'll be scared enough to –'

'By the time we kill the second one, all the others will be there, ready to attack. And it would take away any chance of parleying with them… You never know… They think we broke the rice wine oath by looking for Grabot, but I don't think they're very sure; we'll have to see… Besides, they're even stronger in the jungle than they are here.'

'If we're going to die, we might as well kill a few of them. Two can get in through this hole and four, five, six, eight, no more than that, on the other side. The odds are good. What if we made a run for it that way? There's only the barricade.'

'And what about the jungle?'

Claude fell silent again. Perken was listening: the sound of a cauldron being rolled reached them.

'They won't try the fire before dark,' he went on. 'Our only chance is to make a run for it at nightfall. Take advantage of the darkness, before –'

'All the same, I'd really enjoy killing a few of them! That one strolling over there on his own, my revolver will make his hair stand on end… Are you sure we can't take care of him?' He indicated the bullets in the chamber. 'There'll still be two left…'

'Oh, yeah?'

That was Grabot. So a voice, a voice alone, could express so much hate. This man was here with them. And there wasn't just hate in his voice, there was certainty. Claude looked at him in dismay: his skin was discoloured, like a man who had been locked in a cellar, but his shoulders were those of a fighter… A powerful ruin. And he had been more than courageous. He, too, was decaying beneath the weight of Asia, like the temples… A man who had dared to destroy one of his own eyes, and had tried to enter a region like this alone, without any safeguards. 'If things go badly, they still can't go any further than my revolver…' Terror hovered over him, at that moment, as much as it did over the Mois.

'Good God, it's surely not impossible to –'

'Idiot!'

Much more than the insult, more even than the voice, Grabot's ravaged head was saying: you can't do it when it's pointless, and when it's necessary, it sometimes happens that you can't do it any more… 'All you have to do is want it…' Claude felt out of place in all this… His hand turned out, the barrel pointing towards his head, he lifted his revolver, even though he sensed how absurd it was, even though he knew that if he had fired, he would have turned the gun, at the last moment, on Grabot, to eliminate that face, that hatred, that presence – to chase away that evidence of his own condition as a man, like a murderer chopping off his own telltale finger. He suddenly felt the weight of the revolver and let his hand drop. The absurdity streamed out of him like fast-running water, and for the first time the sinister shadows on the other side of the clearing, the spears and the savage horns highlighted against the sky, seemed to have no force. The impression lasted a moment, then one of the Mois stood up, almost fell as he did so, and clutched at his neighbour, who cried out. The sound, muffled by distance, slowly crossed the clearing and woke it from its paralysed, siegelike state. On the other side, the Mois were increasing in number. But whether crouching or moving, armed with crossbows or spears, they always stopped at the edge of the clearing, packed together, swarming like dogs or wolves behind that mysterious line, as if some occult power were forbidding them to cross it. The only thing alive in the empty clearing, overpowering everything, was time: the minutes were imprisoned within that circle of brutes, who were taking on a timeless character, as if nothing could ever again arrive from the outside world across that barrier of heads, as if, for the white men, living through these hours – including the hour foreshadowed by the draining of colour from the sky, the hour of nightfall which would soon be followed by the fire – simply meant enduring ever more irrefutably the oppressiveness of that human barrier in front of the other barrier of giant stakes, and understanding ever more clearly that this imprisonment was a preparation for slavery. They had been run to earth: like the heads of wild animals lying in wait, those heads lived only through their eyes, which converged on the hut as if on the centre of a trap. Whenever Claude stared at one of the heads in the circle of the binoculars, the first thing he saw was the eyes, like the eyes of greedy animals. When he lowered the binoculars, the eyes vanished in the distance, but he could still see those screwed-up eyelids, those necks stretching like the necks of dogs.

More warriors had appeared, leaning on their crossbows, as if their companions had been duplicated. They were advancing like ants, still along that mysterious line, towards the left. The wall of the hut hid them: Perken made a hole in it. Almost beneath his eyes, a grave surmounted by two big jagged fetishes: a man and a woman, gripping their own sexual organs, which were painted red. Beyond it, a hut. It was clear now that the Mois were moving behind that hut, which they intended to occupy: but as trellises had been placed across its openings, no movement could be seen inside it. The line of Mois disappeared behind it as if falling through a trapdoor: they were gradually approaching, and each time they became invisible, it was because they had moved closer to that façade, as closed and alive with humming as a wasps' nest, beyond those two wooden sexual organs with the shrivelled fingers embedded in them. The façade, too, was alive, insidious, motionless, charged with everything that was hidden in it, those subhuman men who were disappearing behind it suddenly transformed into a menacing absence…

'What do they gain by doing that?' Claude whispered. 'Coming closer?'

'Perhaps there aren't so many of them…' Perken took the binoculars again. Almost immediately he made a gesture with his hand in the air, as if to call Claude, but moved his hand back to stop the binoculars moving. Then he passed them to him. 'Look at the corners.'

'Well?'

'Lower down, near the floor.'

'What's bothering you? The things being passed or the kinds of holes?'

'It's the same: the things are crossbows, the holes are there to pass others through.'

'So what?'

'There are more than twenty.'

'When we start shooting, the trellises won't protect those fellows!'

'They're lying down. We'll lose a lot of bullets. Apart from that, it'll be dark. They'll see us because this hut'll be burning, but we'll see almost nothing.'

'So why all this fuss? They only had to stay where they were.'

'They want us alive.'

Claude looked, fascinated, at the enormous trap, the size of it, the curved wooden crossbows emerging from its base like mandibles. He barely heard what Xa was saying to Perken, who took the binoculars again. Claude now looked in the same direction, to the edge of the clearing. Many of the Mois had bent towards the ground as if bedding plants: the others were walking very carefully, bending their knees and lifting their feet high, like cats. He turned to Perken, questioningly.

'They're planting spikes.'

So they were definitely waiting for night, and making their preparations. What else were they doing behind the hut, behind the milling line of bent bodies?

There was no point even thinking about stopping the Mois from burning down their hut: once the fire was lit, they could do nothing but rush forwards – towards the crossbows – or to the right, towards the spikes. Beyond, the stakes of the perimeter fence, and beyond that, the jungle… There was nothing to be done, except kill as many as possible. Oh, those leeches that sizzled as they twisted on matches!

The only thing they could do was what Perken had advised: try to get away at nightfall, just before the fire. There was still the jungle… But what chance was there of getting that far with the spikes there?

Claude looked at the carts.

The carts – the stones.

To start again…

Get out of here first, or be killed. They mustn't be taken alive.

'What are they planting now?'

They were bustling again on the other side of the clearing, spears crossed.

'They aren't planting anything. The chief has come back.'

Perken passed the binoculars to Claude again. The agitation, seen close up, remained ordered: nothing could distract the Mois from their goal. The extreme tension of the atmosphere, the hostility that hung in the air, as if all the gestures made in their direction had gathered in one soul: everything converged from those men watching and waiting towards these men driven into a corner. And something in the hut itself was suddenly in harmony with that relentless soul: Perken. He stood motionless, fixed as if in a snapshot, staring into the distance, open-mouthed, all his features sagging. Nothing human was left in the hut. Xa had collapsed in his corner, and was waiting, huddled like a wild animal. Grabot – if only he would continue to keep quiet! – around them, those bestial faces, that sadistic instinct, specific and brutal, like the *gaur* skull with its corpse-like teeth. And Perken was turned to stone. The horror of man crushed by solitude seized Claude in the pit of the stomach and the curve of the hips, the horror of man abandoned among madmen who were about to make their move. He did not dare speak, but touched Perken on the shoulder: Perken pushed him away without looking at him, took two steps forward and stopped in the doorway – an easy target for arrows.

'Be careful!'

Perken had stopped listening. So, this life, already long, was going to end here, in a pool of warm blood, or in this disease of courage which had led to Grabot's downfall, as if nothing anywhere could escape the jungle. He looked at him: his head bowed on his chest, his face hidden by his hair, the blind man was walking slowly in circles – as if around the millstone – one shoulder thrust forward, back in his slave state. Perken was haunted by his own face, as he himself might be tomorrow, never again able to open his eyes… But they could still fight. They could kill! This jungle wasn't just an intractable profusion, it was full of trees and bushes from behind which you could shoot – or die of hunger. The nagging madness of hunger, which, he knew, was preferable to the millstones sleeping in the village, with their harness of slaves. In the jungle, you could at least kill yourself in peace.

It was impossible to think clearly in the presence of those waiting heads: the insurmountable humiliation of man hunted down by his own destiny shone forth. The struggle against decay exploded inside him, like a sexual fury, exacerbated by Grabot, who was still going round in circles in the hut as if around the corpse of his own courage. He was gripped by a ridiculous idea: he recalled the punishments reserved in hell for pride – limbs broken and turned inside out, the head lolling back like a sack, the body for ever planted in the earth like a stake – and desperately wanted all that to exist so that a man could at last spit in the face of torture, his consciousness and will intact, even as he was screaming. He felt such a fierce sense of joy at the thought of gambling with more than his own death, it became so much his revenge on the universe, his liberation from the state of being human, that he felt as if he were struggling against a bewitching madness, as if he were suddenly inspired. The words 'No man holds out against torture' crossed his mind, but they had no force, they were just a phrase, underlined by an inexplicable clicking: his teeth were chattering. He jumped onto the trellis, hesitated for a moment, fell, got up again, with one arm in the air, holding his revolver by the barrel, like a ransom.

'Has he gone mad?' Claude, holding his breath, followed him with the barrel of his weapon: Perken was walking towards the Mois, slowly and stiffly. The low sun cast long diagonal shadows across the clearing, and the grip of the revolver gleamed in the fading light. Perken could not see a thing. His feet hit a low bush, and he made a gesture with his hand, as if to push it aside – he was not following the path. He continued moving forward, fell to one knee, stood up again, as stiff as before, without letting go of the revolver. The plants stung so much that he saw, for a moment, what was in front of him: the chief bending his hand to the earth, obstinately. He had to put down the revolver. It was up there in his hand. Finally managed to bend his arm, and took the weapon with his other hand, as if to pull it away. This wasn't hesitation any more: he was unable to move. Finally his hand came down abruptly and opened, the fingers outstretched. The revolver fell to the ground.

A few more steps. He had never before walked like this, without bending his knees. The strength that lifted him underestimated what his bones could do: without the will that was drawing him towards torture with the power of a fascinated animal, he would surely have veered off course. Each step of his stiff legs echoed in the small of his back and his neck. Each blade of grass torn out by his feet, which he could not see, pinned him to the ground, strengthened his body's resistance, one foot following another, with a vibration that was cut off by the following step. As he came closer, the Mois lowered their spears towards him: they glittered vaguely in the dying light. It suddenly occurred to him that most likely they didn't just blind their slaves, but castrated them too.

Once more he found himself rooted to the spot, defeated by his own flesh, his own entrails, by everything that could rebel against man. It wasn't fear: he knew he would continue his bull-like walk. So destiny could do more than just destroy his courage: Grabot was almost certainly a corpse twice over. He had a beard, though... Absurdly, he tried to turn and have another look at him. But all he could see was the revolver.

The weapon was very close to the path, almost in the centre of a patch of bare clay, as if it had burnt the earth around it. It could kill seven of these men. It could defend them all. It was alive. He walked back towards it. The curved wooden crossbows shone for a moment in the red air of the clearing.

It was clear now that there was a world of atrocities beyond those gouged eyes, that castration he had just discovered... There was madness, too, like the endless jungle beyond the edge of the clearing... But he wasn't mad yet: he was overcome by a tragic elation, an irrepressible joy. He kept his eyes on the ground: his torn gaiters and twisted leather laces reminded him, absurdly, of the old image of a barbarian chief, a prisoner like him, thrown alive into a barrel of vipers, and screaming his war song as he died, his fists brandished like broken knots… Horror and resolve clung to his skin. He kicked at the revolver, which travelled a metre, bouncing drunkenly from grip to barrel, like a toad. He resumed his walk towards the Mois.

Claude, breathless, held him in the circle of the binoculars as if he had him in the sights of a rifle. Were the Mois going to open fire? He tried to see them, but could not immediately adjust to the change of distance, and without delay he moved his binoculars back onto Perken, who had resumed exactly the same walking position, his chest thrust forward: a man without arms, back bent like someone towing a boat, stiff legs. When he had turned, for a moment, Claude had glimpsed his face again, so quickly that all he had seen was the open mouth, but he could guess how fixed the eyes were from the stiffness of the body, the shoulders slowly moving forward with the force of a machine. The circle of the binoculars eliminated everything, except this man. The field of vision shifted to the left: he hit the binoculars with his wrist to bring it back to where it had been. Once again, he lost Perken. He looked for him further on, in one of the long streaks of sunlight. Perken had come to a standstill.

For a moment, the line of Mois towards whom he was walking had seemed to him to lack substance, their heads clearly visible but the lower parts of their bodies lost in the mist that was beginning to rise from the ground. A last quivering gleam shone on all these things in motion, as if expressing the breathless anguish of men against the peace of the evening. His empty hand was now closing, limply, as light as a sick man's hand, as if he were still searching for a weapon. All at once, looking up at the treetops, which glowed red for a long while in the last rays of the sun, while at ground level the motionless agitation continued, his passion for the freedom he was about to lose overcame him to the point of delirium. On the verge of the ghastly transformation that haunted him, he clutched himself, digging his tense fingers into the flesh of his thighs, his eyes too small to take in everything he could see, his skin like a nerve. Flung sexually onto this dying freedom, lifted up by a fanatical will possessing itself before this imminent destruction, he was plunging into death itself, his gaze fixed on the horizontal rays ever lengthening up above, freed from those sinister, futile shadows hidden in the darkness that rose from the earth. The red light of the sun lengthened suddenly, like a shadow, and the disintegrating daylight that preceded night in the Tropics by a few moments descended on the clearing. The shapes of the Mois became blurred, except for the line of spears, black against the lifeless sky, from which the redness had disappeared. Perken was falling into the hands of the men, face to face with these forms full of hate, the savage appearance of these spears. And suddenly, everything was turned upside down, he heard himself crying out and felt as if hands had seized him. No: he hadn't been touched, it was just fear, and the sensation was fading, but it hurt as if he had been hit… At last, with the smell of grass filling his nostrils, he understood what had happened: he had stumbled over a spike, and had fallen onto other spikes. Blood flowed from a torn wrist. He lifted himself first onto his hands: he must have been wounded in the knee. The Mois had barely moved, although they were a little closer to him… Had they been about to throw themselves on him, had they been stopped? In the semi-darkness, all he could see distinctly was the whites of their eyes, darting here and there but obstinately returning to him. A herd. So close… If one of them jumped, he could easily spear him. The pain came back, both sharp and numbing, but he felt as if he had been delivered from himself: he was coming back to the surface. The Mois were holding their spears in both hands, across their chests, as if approaching their prey. And he was breathing like a wild animal. In his pocket, he still had his little Browning; should he shoot the chief, without getting it out? But what then? Impossible to lean on his wounded leg. Resting on the other, he let it droop, but the weight of the foot pulled it down, and he felt a shooting pain in his knee: it rose at regular intervals, dull but piercing, like the blood beating in his temples and echoing in his head. And suddenly there was a lot of movement around him: he became aware of it as if it had been summoned by the pain. The Mois had moved closer behind him, separating him from Claude. Was that the only reason they had let him come this far?

4

He stood there in front of them. The chief could not take his eyes off him, his eyelids quivering, which made it look as if he were blinking, waiting for him to make his next move. In his good right hand, Perken still held the little Browning, ready to fire through the material, hampered however by a reflex which forced him to hold the pocket up, as if in so doing he could take some weight off the wounded leg. He stretched his left hand towards the guide, who was standing next to the chief. The savage lifted his sabre at an angle towards this advancing hand, but he realised that the gesture was a peaceful one: the sabre almost touched his hand – from which the blood was dripping noiselessly to the ground – and then was lowered.

'Do you know that man is worth a hundred jars?' Perken cried.

The guide did not translate, and Perken's sense of his own powerlessness struck him like a revelation. If only he could take the brute by the neck and shake him, make him speak!

'Translate, for God's sake!'

The guide was looking at him, his head buried between his shoulders, as if he were more afraid of these words than he was to fight. Perken guessed that he did not understand: he had spoken too quickly, in uninflected Siamese, and the fact that he had shouted the words made it all the more difficult to distinguish the tones.

He started again, forcing himself to slow down. 'You tell chief…'

He separated the words, exasperated by his own rushed breathing, which beat out the syllables. His eyes fixed on those of the interpreter, feeling awkward in front of this savage, he tried to read his mind. The Moi slowly leant his shoulder towards the chief, as if he was going to speak.

'…Blind white man worth…'

Did he understand? His, Perken's, destiny, was being played out against this living block. His life had ended up here, up against these legs covered with eczema, this vile, bloodstained loincloth, this human being capable only of snares and cunning, like the beasts of the jungle. He was totally dependent on this creature, with his wormlike mind. At that moment, there was something coming to life, silently, in that head, like flies' eggs hatching in the brain. He had not felt such a strong desire to kill anyone for the past hour.

'…worth more than a hundred jars…'

At last, he was translating! The old chief did not move. Everyone was so still that it seemed as if the only thing that had not come to a halt was the night, which could be seen rising towards the sky. Just as it had during that morning's ritual, the whole life of this place isolated from the world hung on the silent shadow of the chief. Not even the cry of an animal could be heard from the depths of the leaves, which, in this silence, this immobility, seemed to stretch to the ends of the earth. Perken was waiting for some gesture, but instead, the chief leant towards the interpreter, and said something. The man immediately translated.

'More than a hundred?'

'More.'

The chief was thinking, constantly moving his teeth like a rabbit. He lifted his head: a cry had just reached them from the other side of the clearing.

'Perken!'

Claude had lost sight of him and was calling him. In a few minutes, it would be dark. This exchange was their last chance, and if it failed, they would be lost...

'Over here!' Perken shouted at the top of his voice.

The chief was looking at him, suspiciously, still moving his gums, threatening in the silence that had descended again.

'I'm calling him,' Perken said to the interpreter.

'No gun!' the chief replied.

'Just bring the little Browning,' Perken cried in French.

The fight wasn't over...

A circle of light appeared in the grey gloom into which the voice had vanished: Claude had turned his torch on. He himself was invisible, and there was not the slightest sound of bushes being trampled, but the circle kept advancing in a zigzagging motion, always at the same height, keeping company with the liquid throbbing of the blood in Perken's temples, which he could not shake off. The light was following the path, without any doubt. Suddenly, it lifted away from the ground, swept like a scythe over the gathered men, then returned to the ground to search for the track: all these creatures who had emerged for a moment from the gloom – the white tips of the teeth lit suddenly, the torsos leaning towards Perken – became shadows again.

Perken's body was starting to hurt. With some difficulty, he sat down on the ground. The shooting pains became less frequent. The torch went out: Claude was barely a few metres away now, crushing leaves as he advanced. Perken, his legs stretched out, his head near the ground, could see nothing but the mass of the jungle, into which all nearby forms had vanished, and the grille of the spears against the sky. He heard muttering around him, like a muffled argument.

'Are you wounded?'

It was Claude.

'No. Well, I am, but not badly. Sit down next to me. And turn that off.'

The Mois had already started making a big fire.

Perken summarised what had been happening.

'You offered them more than a hundred jars… How many warriors are there?'

'Between a hundred and two hundred.'

'They're grumbling about something… What do you think they're saying?'

Indeed, the muttering had continued, more guttural now. Two voices stood out from the others, louder and more affirmative: one was the chief's.

'I think the chief and Grabot's owner are arguing.'

'What's the chief standing up for? The village as a whole?'

'Yes, most likely.'

'What if we offered a jar to each warrior, and five or ten or whatever to the whole village?'

Immediately, Perken made the offer. No sooner had the interpreter translated than the semi-darkness was filled with voices: everyone was talking at once, softly at first, but the talk soon developed into a furious jabbering. The spears were moving now against the sky, riddled with the same stars as the night before. They vanished when the flames of the pyre sprung up, hissing, lashing everything with their irregular beating. As the fire rose, heads appeared, clear in the front rows, shadowy in the back rows: almost all the warriors were there, mad with words, suddenly liberated from the whites. They were all talking for themselves, louder and louder, their arms still but their heads moving. The fire, at regular intervals, swallowed the muffled castanet noise of the words and applied its reddish touches to their old peasant faces. But then, abruptly, faster than the rising of the flames, their fixed gazes – the gazes of hunters – reappeared. The jabbering surrounded a mute circle: within it, the elders, crouching around the chief, their arms very long, like those of monkeys, were taking turns to speak. Claude could not take his eyes off them. He would have liked to be able to translate the expressions on their faces, but gave up: their expressions were as strange to him as the language they spoke.

The interpreter came up to Perken. 'One of you leaves, the other stays until he comes back…'

'No.'

'A man alone can die on the way,' Claude added. 'So, no exchange.'

The Moi went back, knocking against Perken's wounded leg as he did so. Perken almost cried out: the leg went numb again…

The parleying had resumed.

'If the worst comes to the worst,' Claude said.

'No, I know these savages. If they really want it, the elders won't be able to hold out against the village. And the main thing is to gain time. If it were day, there'd be other ways…'

The jabbering suddenly subsided, like birds flying away: everyone was looking at the group of elders. At the same time as their heads turned, their mouths, which had remained open during their neighbours' speeches, closed attentively.

'No other tribe has one jar per person!' Perken cried in Siamese.

The interpreter translated. The chief said nothing. No one moved: the hostile, expectant silence spread like ripples in water. The warriors were watching the chief.

Perken wanted to stand up, but he feared that he would have difficulty walking, which would weaken his argument. 'We won't have any escort,' he cried again. 'The jars...'

The interpreter came to him, and all the heads turned simultaneously.

'...the jars will be brought on carts.'

'No escort.'

He waited after every sentence for it to be translated immediately.

'Three men only.'

'Make the exchange in a clearing of your choice.'

Claude was so accustomed to see white men nodding in agreement that the immobility of these faces, so soon after all heads had turned towards them, offended him like a rejection. 'Surely it'll win them over,' he murmured, 'if they can each have their own!'

'They don't really realise...'

What was happening? Some of the Mois were standing up. Hesitant, their backs still bowed, one arm pointing straight down to the ground where they had been crouching. They were heading for the hut from which the whites had come, their shadows ahead of them. Three, four... They merged into the mass of the trees: only the upper halves of their spears could still be seen against the starry sky... The others waited. The suspense was so contagious that it spread to the white men. Claude waited for the spears to reappear above the undulating line of the trees. Cries reached them, then an enthusiastic clamour in response. The tips of the spears emerged for a moment, crossed, close to a very bright star, descended, ascended again, grew bigger as they approached. The men entered the red light, connected to the night by their shadows, which were lost in the darkness. Among them, Perken recognised Grabot's master: he had gone to make sure his slave was still there, and the others had feared he had run away. He wanted to return to the hut. Two warriors were holding him by the wrists, and all three were shouting, but Perken could not understand them. At last, they crouched, and the discussions resumed. Again, an absurd atmosphere fell, as if these were peasants debating rather than fierce warriors – not that their ferocity was completely hidden.

'How long is this going on?' Claude asked.

'Until dawn, when they extinguish the pyre. That's always the hour for important decisions.'

Now that his energy was no longer being applied, Perken was falling back on himself. He did not really feel as if he had regained his life: when he had risked torture and degradation, fearing all the while that he would not be able to resist them, he had felt as if he were torn in two, as if there was nothing ahead of him but a kind of fog. Was there anything real in this murmur that rose and fell with the flames, in this gathering of madmen amid the implacable, overpowering presence of the jungle and the night? With the fever, hatred of man overwhelmed him, hatred of life, hatred of all these forces which were again dominating him, gradually dispelling his terrible memories, like the memory of ecstasy. He had stopped feeling like a prisoner, although he was paying more attention to his wound, his shooting pains, his fever, than to his mind. But the bathlike warmth in his cheeks and temples broke down whatever came from men. The Mois had stopped moving. The light of the fire gleamed on the same spears planted in the earth, the same arms glistening with sweat. The noise passed over the assembled men, almost all of them lost in the shadows, like the rustling of insects over crouching mummies. As the pyre died down, the darkness returned, sweeping over them like surf, from which the jumbled spears emerged. The ever-rising fever made them seem as motionless as stones. The night rose to attack this shattered group of savages, covering them as the jungle had covered the temples, then the wave of darkness receded and the heads reappeared, with the fixed red points of their eyes reflecting the fire deep in the night.

Dawn.

A lump of earth was thrown on the pyre, extinguishing the last embers. The interpreter came and crouched beside Perken.

'You choose the time and the place.'

'On oath?'

'On oath.'

He translated in a loud voice.

One by one the Mois stood up, like the remains of a shipwreck in the pale, cold dawn. The group undulated like a tarpaulin, before at last breaking up. Several urinated where they stood.

'Do you believe in the oath, Perken?'

'Wait. I need the cartridges which are in my old holster, in the first cart, under the jacket... My Colt, too.'

'Where is it?'

'I don't know... Somewhere between the hut and here...'

Fortunately, it had fallen in the patch where no grass grew, and Claude found it immediately. As soon as he had picked it up – a proof they were being left in peace – a dressed man came out of their hut: Xa. They walked together to the carts. Xa took out the holster, then came back to Perken.

'What about Grabot?' Perken asked.

The boy raised his outstretched hands. 'Now, asleep!'

The elders had crouched down beneath the *gaur*. A slave brought the jars of alcohol. Perken stood up, leaning on Claude, who was worried by the hollowness and the quivering of his unshaven cheeks: he was biting himself hard to stop himself grimacing with pain. The chief drank, and held out the bamboo reed. Perken moved his head closer, then stopped. Everyone was looking at him.

'What's the matter?' Claude asked.

'Wait…'

Was he going to refuse the oath? The Mois were waiting for a signal from the chief. Perken had raised his left hand, to call for attention. He pulled the Colt from its holster, said to the interpreter, 'Look at the *gaur*', and aimed. It was hard to keep the target within his sights: the fever, and his wound… As long as the night's dew hadn't jammed the mechanism… It was greased… In the early morning light, all eyes were on the bone, polished by the sun and the ants. Perken fired. A patch of blood appeared between the two horns, and grew in size from the centre towards the edges. A red rivulet hesitated, descended suddenly towards the nose, stopped at the edge, and at last fell, drop by drop. The chief held out his hand fearfully. A red drop, hung up there, motionless. It fell on his finger. He immediately licked it, and said something which caused all eyes to turn back to the ground, trapped by a new anxiety.

'A man's blood?' the interpreter asked.

'Yes…'

Claude was waiting for Perken to explain, but Perken was watching the Mois. Their shoulders thrust forward, their bodies sagging and tense at the same time, they moved closer together. From time to time one of them cast a furtive look at the skull, then quickly looked away again. Beneath the darting eyes, the growing dread, the patch seemed to be spreading. On the upper edge, the blood was drying, but another rivulet zigzagged softly down towards the ground. This flow of blood, these rivulets stretching like paws seemed as alive as a large insect, leaving their mark on the skull – almost blue in the light – as if branding it.

With his hand, smeared with blood where his tongue had licked it, the chief indicated the bamboo reed. Perken drank. Claude had hoped they would all suddenly bow down in adoration. 'They're too familiar with the supernatural,' Perken said.

'They look at me the way white men would look at someone who owned an unusually good rifle. And fear me in the same way. But the advantage for us is that now the rice wine oath will be even more binding.'

Claude drank in his turn. 'But what did you do?'

'I filled one of my hollow bullets with blood from my knee.'

The chief stood up. Xa went to harness the bullocks to the carts. Perken and Claude returned to the hut. Grabot was still there, lying on his side, asleep, his arm stretched out, his hand half open. Perken woke him, and told him about the agreement he had come to with the Mois. He was sitting now, his head lolling on his shoulders, saying nothing: he was either hostile or still half asleep.

'I'm sure they won't betray the rice wine oath now,' Perken said.

Grabot opened his hand without replying. Claude turned away his eyes: Xa was advancing with the carts, the last guide beside him. It had not taken him any longer than usual to harness the bullocks, for nothing had been stolen. The way things were resuming their normal course, the way the tragic events of the night were fading, made Claude suddenly aware of his own insignificance. Beneath the *gaur* the space had been cleared. At the extremity of each of the two black rivulets, on the jagged edge of the bone, a drop of blood, glistening in the sun, was coagulating.

5

The guide indicated the Siamese village with his spear: three hundred metres further on, against a patch of jungle, near some banana trees, a group of straw huts, close together, looking like forest animals standing there for all eternity. As far as the horizon, the diminishing, almost parallel lines of the hills: Siam. The guide planted his spear in the ground to mark the spot where the exchange would take place.

'He's chosen well,' Claude said. 'From here you can see all the paths leading up to it.'

Perken, lying on a cart from which Xa had removed the roof, as if on a stretcher, lifted himself. 'He's a fool. If the Siamese plan to act, they won't do it till after the exchange. It won't be difficult to get someone to follow the carts with the jars. And the same man will then guide the militia…'

The Moi was still holding the spear. At last, certain that the white men had understood him, he turned and went back the way he had come, slowly at first, then running, with the awkwardness of a hunted animal. They could no longer hear his steps but could still feel his presence: he was going back towards the savages, like a boat towards a ship.

They were alone with their stones and their carts, alone on this path that impelled them towards the village, whose roofs glittered beyond the chasm of light.

Some of the villagers spoke Siamese. Perken chose drivers, and, day in, day out, they resumed their journey, changing drivers in other villages, as they had in Cambodia. They were moving faster now, to the rhythm of the blood beating in Perken's leg, which was more swollen every day, and in his knee, which was becoming redder and redder. Perken hardly ate, and only got up when he had to. The fever was always worst at night. At last they saw the horns and the high white bells of a pagoda, blue in the tropical light: the first Siamese town. As soon as they got to the bungalow, Xa made enquiries. There was a young native doctor here, who had studied in Singapore and usually lived in Bangkok, as well as an English doctor on his rounds, who would be in town for another two days. 'He eats at the Chinaman's…' It was just after midday. Claude ran to the Chinese eating house. Beneath a *panka*[4], in front of walls of peeling matting hung with huge cigarette advertisements, between soda bottles and greenish jars, a back clad in a white jacket, white hair.

'Doctor?' ·

The man turned slowly. He was holding beansprouts between chopsticks. His face was almost as white as his hair, and his expression as he looked at Claude was both exhausted and resigned. 'What is it now?'

'A white man, seriously wounded. The wound is poisoned.'

The old man slowly shrugged his shoulders and resumed eating. Claude waited a few moments, then made up his mind and placed his fists on the table. The doctor looked up. 'Couldn't you at least let me finish my meal?'

Claude hesitated. 'Should I give him a good slapping?' He was the only European doctor. He sat down at the next table, between the man and the door.

'"I understand" would have been a shorter answer. Go on, finish.'

At last the doctor stood up. 'Where did you put him?'

'Where were you stupid enough to put him?' his voice and face implied.

'In the bungalow.'

'Let's go.'

The sun, the sun…

As soon as he entered the bedroom, he sat down on the bed and opened his knife to cut the breeches, but the leg was so swollen that Perken had already cut them himself down the side. The doctor ripped the material open, but his gestures changed as soon as he started to palpate the patient. The wound, a big, puckered black spot, seemed to bear no relation to his huge red knee.

'Can you bend your knee?'

'No.'

'Were you shot with an arrow?'

'I fell on a spike.'

'How long ago?'

'Five days.'

'That's bad…'

'The Stiengs never poison their spikes.'

'If the spike had been poisoned, you'd have been dead by now. But a man is perfectly capable of poisoning himself. Really good at it, in fact.'

'I put iodine on it… though not right away…'

'You wasted your time, the wound's too deep.' He gently palpated the bright knee, with such a sensitive touch that it felt elastic to Perken. 'It's a tough one… The kneecap is rotating… Give me the thermometer… 38.8… And of course it goes up at night. Are you eating at all?'

'No.'

'The Stiengs, eh?' He shrugged his shoulders again and seemed to be thinking, then he looked at Perken again, resentfully. 'Couldn't you have settled for a quiet life?'

Perken looked at the doctor's pale face. 'When an opium fiend talks me to about a quiet life, I always tell him to lie down. If it's time for your pipe, you'd be better off going now and coming back later after you've smoked it.'

'I'm not asking you –'

'You've heard of Perken, haven't you?'

'What's that to do with you?'

'I'm Perken. So I advise you to take care.'

'To think you could have had it so easy!' He bent again over the wound, not out of obedience, but as if he were looking for something: he was still pursuing his own train of thought. 'Foolishness,' he muttered, 'such foolishness.' His thin smile faded, then returned, a smile of disgust, which lowered the corners of his mouth instead of raising them. 'So you're Perken, eh?'

'No, I'm the Shah of Persia!'

'And you think it matters, do you, that you did things in this country, moved all over, instead of sticking to a quiet life and…'

'Am I asking you if it matters to have a quiet life, as you put it?'

The smile had vanished again. 'All right, Mr Perken, listen carefully. You have suppurated arthritis in the knee. Within two weeks, you're going to die like an animal. And there's nothing we can do about it, do you understand? Absolutely nothing.'

Perken's first instinct had been to hit him, but there was so much more bitterness than hostility in the doctor's voice that he did not move. He sensed in it an old addict's distaste for action…

'We really ought to find a more reliable doctor,' Claude said.

'Don't you believe me?'

Perken reflected. 'Before I saw you, I had a feeling it was something like this. There's an old relationship between death and me…'

'Don't talk nonsense!'

'…but I don't trust you.'

'You ought to. There's nothing we can do. Nothing. Smoke, it'll calm you down, and you won't think of anything else. The opium round here is quite good… When the pain gets too strong, inject yourself… I'll give you one of my syringes. Are you an addict?'

'No.'

'Of course not! Anyway, if you triple the dose as you wish, you'll be able to end it all when you want to… I'll give the boy the syringe.'

'I've already been wounded by the spikes…'

'Not in the knee… The bacterial toxins which are forming inside it will slowly poison you to death. The only solution is amputation, but you don't have time to get to a town where they could carry it out. Inject yourself and think of something else. Keep calm, it'll make a change for you! That's all.'

'Can't you cut it open?'

'We wouldn't get through to anything. The infection is too deep, and the bones are in the way. But if you want to, do as this young man suggests, and send for the Siamese doctor. I warn you he has no clinical experience. And he's a native… But I suppose you prefer these people to us…'

'At the moment, very much so…'

As he was leaving the room, with Xa beside him, the doctor turned, and looked again at Perken and Claude.

'Don't you have anything?'

'No.'

'Because, while I'm here…'

But it was on Perken that his gaze rested: like a reflection in a blurred mirror, his thoughts could be surmised from the heaviness of that gaze, the way he screwed up his eyes. At last he left.

'Pity a good slapping means so little here,' Claude said. 'What a character! Shall I go and find the Siamese doctor?'

'Straight away. Any white doctor on his rounds in this region is bound to be a character: addicted either to opium or to sex… Xa, go and find the station chief and give him this.' He held out a Siamese administrative document in which the only thing written in Latin characters was his own name. 'Tell him it's from Perken. And find me some women for tonight.'

When Claude returned – the native doctor would be along soon – the station chief was there. Perken and he were talking in Siamese: the official listened, gave brief replies, and took notes. Under dictation, he wrote down a dozen sentences.

'So, what about Grabot?' Claude asked, as soon as he had left.

'We'll get him back. This fellow thinks, as I do, that the government will take the opportunity to send in the militia to quell the rebellion, and to occupy everything they can in rebel country. It's a good excuse, and a real advantage. A white man tortured – the French can't complain, and one day they might find an excuse of that kind, which would be unfortunate. The people who hold the railway concession are strongly in favour of military occupation… He took down the text of my dispatch, we'll have an answer this evening. If the soldiers start by blowing up a village, it'll spread panic throughout the region…'

Claude had raised the matting a little and was looking at the path through the window, which had no pane. No one in sight. When was the Siamese doctor going to get here? The palms were swallowed up in the sky, of a blue as incandescent as mercury lighting. The sun hit the ground with such force, it seemed to put an end to all life. This was not the trance of the jungle: here, the heat was slowly taking possession of the earth and of men, establishing its implacable domination. In this heat everything – plans, human will – vanished into thin air. As the heat and the renewed silence pervaded the room, another presence rose from the blinding whiteness of the ground, from the sleeping animals, from the immobility of the two men who had taken refuge in this overheated shade: death. While the Englishman had been here, Perken had been more concerned with answering him than with understanding. Later, he had forced himself into action, postponing the moment when that thought, which was all around him like the dazzle of the sun, returned. Now at last it had caught up with him.

He was not convinced by the doctor's calm assertion, and, despite what he had said, he was not convinced by his own feelings either, now that he was making more of an effort to grasp them. He was used to wounds. He knew about fever, the sporadic pain that contorted his knee: that was where his sickness was, in that sensitivity that was like an abscess, in those reflexes of swollen flesh recoiling nervously from the smallest object, not in the poisoning of his blood, which he could not feel. The only thing that could combat the assertion of the wound was the assertion of men: his ability to gain control of his own life depended on the Siamese doctor.

No sooner had he entered than everything collapsed, as if Perken had been woken with a jolt: the doctor's professional indifference was enough to destroy this world of defences. Perken felt suddenly separated from his own body, that irresponsible body which was trying to drag him down into death. The doctor undid the bandage and examined the wound, crouching Siamese-style by the bed. Perken enumerated the symptoms he had already told the English doctor about. The Siamese said nothing in reply, but continued palpating him with great dexterity. Perken was not so much fearful as impatient: he was confronting an enemy again, even if this enemy was his own blood.

'On the way here, Monsieur Perken, I met Doctor Blackhouse. He's not a very… moral man, but he's an experienced doctor. He told me, with that English contempt of his – as if I knew nothing about this illness – that it was suppurated arthritis. I've read about it in the manuals, it was widespread during the European war, but I've never encountered it before. You have all the symptoms. To combat an infectious disease of this nature, amputation would be necessary. But in the present state of science…'

Perken raised his hands, cutting short the speech. This westernised gibberish reminded him that he was being given this cautious confirmation of his death in expectation of a just reward. He paid, and the man left. He watched him as he went – as if that were proof.

He believed more in the threat of death than in death itself: at once imprisoned in his own flesh and separate from it, like those men who were drowned after being tied to corpses. He was such a stranger to this death lurking within him that he felt as if he were gearing up again for a fight. But the look in Claude's eyes cast him back into his body. It was a look of intense complicity, a mixture of compassion and the heart-rending fraternity of courage, the deep animal feeling that united men when the body was doomed. To Perken, although he felt a stronger connection with him than with any other creature, it seemed as if his death were coming from Claude. The strongest assertion of it was not in the words of the doctors, but in the way Claude had instinctively lowered his eyes. There was another shooting pain in his knee, and his leg contracted in a reflex: a harmony was becoming established between the pain and death, as if one had become the inevitable preparation for the other. Then the wave of pain receded, taking with it the will that had fought against it. But it was only lying dormant, ready to strike again. For the first time he had the sense of something inside him that was stronger than himself, something against which no hope could prevail. But he'd have to fight that, too…

'What's surprising, Claude, in the presence of death, even… even if it's a long way away, is that you know immediately what you want, you can't hesitate any more…'

They looked at each other, submitting to that silent bond they had felt several times before. Perken had sat down on the bed, his leg stretched out. His eyes were sharper again now, but full of awareness, as if his will could not help clinging to old regrets.

Claude tried to read his thoughts. 'Do you want to go back up there with the militia?'

Perken hesitated, surprised: the idea hadn't occurred to him. To his mind, the Stiengs were not responsible for his death... 'No, I need men now. I have to go back to my territory.'

All at once, it struck Claude how much older than him Perken was. It wasn't his face, or his voice: it was as if the years hung heavy on him, like a faith. They were irremediably different from each other, of two different races...

'What about the stones?'

'Right now, there's nothing worse than the things that once gave us hope...'

Could he get back to his mountains alone?

There was nothing now to stop Claude from reaching Bangkok.

Nothing, except the presence of death.

'I'll go with you.'

Silence. As if to free themselves from the grip of such a rare union between men, both looked at the window, blinded by the light outside which glittered beneath the matting. The minutes passed, burnt by the motionless sun. Claude thought of the stones sheltered beneath the roofs of the carts, emptied of the life which had made them struggle so fiercely against him. If he left them in this station, he would find them again. And if he didn't find them... 'Why have I decided to go with him?' He couldn't abandon him, either to other human beings, from whom he felt for ever separated, or to death. The exercise of a power he had yet to discover drew him like a revelation: it was through such decisions, and only through them, that he could nourish the contempt that separated him from everything that other people accepted. Whether he came out a winner or a loser, this game could not help making him more of a man, assuaging his need for courage, his consciousness of the vanity of the world and the pain of men which he had so often seen, in an unformed state, in his grandfather... The matting was noise-lessly moved aside, casting a swirl of triangular atoms into the room. It seemed to him that his reason, so fragile and derisory, was being swallowed in this mass of air, that the only thing in himself that mattered was his will.

A barefoot native was bringing a telegram, the provisional response received by the station chief: '*Prepare billets, base of action militia to quell rebellion eight hundred men machine guns.*'

'Eight hundred men,' Perken said. 'They're planning to pacify the region... As far as where?... Even if I hadn't already made up my mind, I'd have to go back up there... And they have machine guns...'

Xa came back in. 'Mssié, women...'

'Way to find one for me, too?' Claude asked.

'Way.'

They both went out.

Two women were standing to the right of the door. The smaller one was wearing flowers and had soft lips: two things that aroused Perken's hostility. He hated languor now. He signalled to the other woman to come, before he had even looked at her. The smaller one left.

The air hung suspended, as if time had stood still, as if the trembling of Perken's fingers were the only thing alive in this silence dominated by the Asian immobility of this face with its thin, curved, nose. His fingers were not trembling with desire, or fever, although he could sense in the intensity of everything around him that the fever was rising: they were trembling like a gambler's. Tonight, he did not fear impotence, but, in spite of the human smell into which he was plunging, he was again gripped by dread.

She lay down, naked, her body hairless and hazy in the gloom. One could make out a tiny growth of pubic hair, and her eyes. They held him, as he searched them in vain for the captivating degeneracy of nakedness. She closed them to escape his domination, which sprang from feelings she could not fathom. Accustomed to the desires of men, but fascinated by the growing intensity, in this absolute silence, of that gaze that would not leave her own, she waited. Forced by the cushions to open her legs and arms slightly, her lips parted, she seemed to create her own desire, to summon her own satisfaction through the slow rising and falling of her breasts. Their movement pervaded the room: repeated over and over, always the same, and always stronger. The breasts fell like a wave, and gradually rose again: the muscles tensed, and all the shadowy hollows of her body deepened. As soon as he put his arm beneath her – she had to help him – he felt the fear leave her. She supported herself on her hip so that she could shift slightly, and for a moment, the yellow light encircled her rump like a whiplash and vanished between her legs. The warmth of her body penetrated him. Suddenly she bit his lips, emphatically underlining, by this tiny intervention of her will, her inability to suppress the rising and falling movement of her breasts.

Ten centimetres from her face with its bluish eyelids, it seemed to him like a mask. He felt almost separate from the savage thrill that pressed him to this body he was possessing as violently as if he were beating it. The whole face, the whole woman, was in her tensed mouth. Suddenly the swollen lips opened and quivered over the teeth, and, as if originating there, a long shiver went all through her taut body, as inhuman and motionless as a tree held in a trance by the heat of the day. The mouth was still the only thing alive in that face, although every time Perken moved he could hear a nail scratching the sheet. Beneath the shiver, which was intense now, she stopped touching the bed and raised her finger in the air. Her mouth closed like an eyelid being lowered. Although the corners of her lips contracted, her body, horrified at itself, was already moving away from him. There was no more hope: never, never would he experience this woman's sensations, never would he find in this frenzy that shook him anything other than the worst kind of separation. You only ever possess what you love. Trapped by her move, not even free to bring her back by clinging to her, he, too, closed his eyes, thrown back on himself as if on a drug, longing to destroy, through violence, that anonymous face that was driving him towards death.

Part Four

I

More nights and more days – death and Claude both beside him – in the heat and the mosquitoes that seemed to rise from his pain-wracked knee, wheeled through the jungle by this torpor, this irregular alternation of rough clearings and vegetation that had replaced the alternation of day and night, this world where now the nights drooped like the leaves – where time itself decayed. The clearings were more frequent now, as if the jungle had at last been torn out and made way for light. But Perken knew that this was the big valley, and that a new wave of jungle would soon close over his motionless body and shattered will, in which hope vanished in the howling of wild dogs and the excruciating burning of insect bites. He had asked for his shoe to be taken off for a moment: the skin was dark red with bites all the way down to where the leather had been, as if it had been tattooed. Over and above the pain, the itching, the decay, the endless cries of the monkeys and the twisted branches which had reappeared before every hole in the jungle ever since they had started climbing again towards Laos, towards *his* territory, it was the fleeing Stiengs who filled the depths which concealed them, like an ultimate decay. Once the jars had been handed over, and Grabot released and taken to hospital in Bangkok, the militia had been sent in to quell the rebellion. With their burden of men wounded by spikes and traps, they had marched on the village, blown up the gate and cleared the huts with grenades, leaving behind them a charnel house, black pigs searching among the pulverised jars, their bellies covered in insects... The fleeing Stiengs had swept through the villages. The militiamen pursuing them had lost a lot of men in the tall jungle, especially from poisoned wounds, so the sick the Stiengs had left behind were treated with grenades, and the wounded with bayonets. The migrating tribesmen bored through the jungle like animals slowly stampeding towards a watering hole, and climbed eastward without disturbing its wrinkled surface, but, in the evenings, long columns of fire, rising straight in the motionless air against the endless receding vista of trees, showed where the tribes had stopped on their epic march.

The fires had started to appear a few days after Claude and Perken had left the Siamese town. Now there were more of them every night as they approached both Perken's territory and the site of the railway, blocking the horizon through every new gap in the jungle. Invisible in the cicada-filled night, the militiamen, and, behind them, the government of Siam... 'Men like me always have to make use of governments,' Perken had said. The government was behind this darkness, chasing away the animal tribes before chasing away the others, pushing its railway line forward kilometre by kilometre, every year burying the corpses of its adventurers a little further up-country. By day, when the columns of smoke appeared, as distinct as tree trunks, they could see between them, through their binoculars, red-painted skulls against the sky. When would the fires, whose crackling seemed muffled in the vastness, reach the path along which they themselves were moving? A long way back, where the railway line was being laid, a searchlight appeared in the sky as soon as the columns of smoke began to vanish in the gloom, as if the great flight of the Mois, rolling in waves through the trees like migrating cattle, had found its centre in the triangle of light projected on the sky by white men. Through a new gap in the trees, a deep landscape started to appear, as if seen from a plane, its plunging lines a long way from the path, the background a dense, saturated blue. The sun suffused this background, shimmering there like something underwater, a vitreous mass on the ridges, but like dust around the palms. In the distance – a few white Buddhist bells in the dark greenery – the first friendly Laotian village, Samrong, the first village whose chief Perken knew, which meant they were getting close to his own territory. Between them and the village, columns of smoke rose in the vastness, making it seem even larger, and their advance was linked so directly to the life of the jungle that it seemed invincible, as if it had come not from men but from the earth, like a fire or a tide.

'Why on earth are they marching on a village where the warriors are armed? They must be forced to…'

'Perhaps they're starving,' Claude said.

'The militia have given up on them now. Their orders are to go no further than the river. Beyond the river is Savan's territory, and beyond that, mine.'

The river with its U-bend shone incandescently in the distance, the only white thing in the blue chasm.

'I have to help Savan defend his village.'

'In your state?'

'If we follow the ridge, we'll be there well before they will. A day's delay at the most…'

He was still looking at the village and the jungle, but, even though he was chewing his nails fiercely in order not to scratch himself, he seemed lost in thought. Claude did not insist: he understood all too well the sense of fraternity that drew him there. And there was a new source of anxiety to keep him silent: as if born out of the tall columns of smoke advancing inexorably across the expanse like genies of the jungle, a succession of hammer blows could be heard from somewhere in the great dormant silence. Too weak to fill this inferno of light, they faded like the occasional birds that rose from the trees and then, horrified by the oppressive sun, immediately fell back in like stones. The regular intervals between these blows swallowed by the light made them sound like a solemn announcement being beaten out on a distant planet. Claude recalled the sound of the nail extractor on the stone.

'Listen…'

'What?' He had been concentrating on his pain, which was receding. He held his breath. One… two… three… four… The blows were more frequent now, distinct but muffled, almost spongy: the slow advance of the columns of smoke emphasised their acceleration.

'There are men there,' Claude said. 'Do you think they're building some kind of entrenchment?'

'It's not the Mois. The columns of smoke are still advancing, and the sound is much closer to us.'

Perken was trying to orient his binoculars according to the sound, but in vain: although the blue heat haze did not conceal the jungle, it blurred its shapes. The shooting pains in his knee started again, like the strokes of a bell, one by one, out of time with the distant blows, and no human form appeared against the vegetation seething with hatred, which itself seemed to be giving rise to these columns of smoke and this inexplicable hammering. Below, a point of light appeared, like a flash of sunlight on a window.

There was no water in that direction.

He looked again, stopped the cart, kept looking. His foot, painful and lifeless at the same time, was in the way of the light. He lifted himself up, without even trying to move his foot: it was just a piece of skin, separate from him – as if he were suffering in someone else's skin. Now he could see. Claude was holding out his hand, but Perken did not pass him the binoculars. The point of light was rising and falling, as intermittent as the rattle of the blows to which they seemed to give birth. Perken let his hand drop, but did not let go of the binoculars. Claude tried to take them. At last, Perken unclenched his fingers.

'But surely the river is that way?' he said.

Claude was staring at the point of light – a cooking pot, a piece of camping equipment? – a long way *in front* of the river.

Quite close, he could see thin lines, crossed, human forms, larger geometric surfaces. He knew what they were: tents. The crossed lines were stacks of weapons. He, too, looked again towards the river: it was a long way behind. And a new point of light sprang up in front, following the Mois' columns of smoke.

'The militia?' Claude asked.

Perken was silent for a moment. 'They also think I'm already dead...'

He was looking alternately at his leg and the light, with a kind of horror. He finally looked away from the leg. The resonant, barrel-like sound of the wooden mallets hitting the tent pegs echoed across the expanse. Gradually, the sound spread and dominated the columns of smoke, the jungle itself, all these things crushed beneath the sun. The will of men was once again in command, and in the service of death. Despite the pain, he felt fiercely alive in opposition to this assertion of his decay. He wanted to resume the fight. And yet everything he had done was there before him, like his own corpse. Within a week, the militia would reach his territory, and he would have spent his whole life waiting in vain.

The stacks were there. The militia were advancing, unconcerned about the great bend in the river, which gave off a phosphorescent, almost electric blue light. The tents were there. And yet he did not feel any certainty, but a kind of anxious nausea, like those moments before vomiting when you almost lose consciousness. Mindful above all, reluctantly, of the pain, which rose and fell like a boat, he was relieved to rediscover the militiamen and death: linked one to the other, both advancing towards their goal like the great columns of smoke.

'It may be,' he thought, 'that making your death is much more important to me now than making your life...'

He raised the binoculars: the village reappeared with surprising clarity, between the two blurred forms of his shoes.

As his life tumbled down over the precipice, the village was there like a stone to which he had to cling – like the stones of the temple. And the binoculars returned, of their own accord, to the militiaman. But one wave was following the other, and he would have to fight the Stiengs first.

'We'll get to Savan's territory a good while before they will…'

'Do you really trust the fellow?'

'No: the only ones I'm sure of are the northern chiefs. But we have no choice…'

2

The increasingly rapid rifle shots, interspersed now with echoes, surrounded Samrong and its Buddhist bells with intermittent points of light, apart from a patch of darkness. Within the almost closed circle, the night cicadas, the reddish light of a lantern: the peace of Laos, heavy and imprisoned.

'Still nothing down there, Claude?' Perken could no longer get up.

Claude looked through the binoculars again. 'I can't see a thing.' He had no sooner put down the binoculars than the flash of another rifle shot appeared, quite close to a hilltop: the report returned as an echo, a tone higher. Another shot. So close to the stars, the flashes of light looked dirty.

'Do you think the Stiengs have surrounded the village?'

'Impossible.' Perken pointed to an indistinct hill. 'Our look-outs haven't started firing over there, which means the Stiengs aren't trying to climb.'

'Mois know where find machine guns near railway,' Xa said.

The fires were quivering like reddish flames, beyond the rifle shots. Perken kept looking at them: if they were still alight, it meant the militia had not reached there yet. A form passed across the field of the binoculars, very close, hiding the one that Perken was examining. 'Who goes there?'

He was lying on boards, looking out over the garden from the height of the piles. The form disappeared. He fired in its direction, haphazardly, and waited for a cry. Nothing.

'That's the second time…'

'Ever since you advised them to stop the militia,' Claude replied, 'things have turned nasty… As long as it was only a question of helping them against the Stiengs…'

'Bunch of idiots!'

The lookouts posted by Perken were firing much more now: the stream of Stiengs who had fought against the militia were now on their way to attack the village.

'Are you sure about what you told them? I'm afraid that if they send mediators, the commander of the militia won't give a damn, and that if they fire, the militia will respond with machine guns…'

'The militia are under orders not to fight them. They're Buddhists, they live a sedentary life, and like my men they're armed. They'll negotiate. But if they let the militiamen in unconditionally, they'll start "administering", as the Siamese say. Savan's the only one who understands that… But his authority as a chief is as uncertain as those rifle shots… There's nothing to discuss: if they get in here, the way will be open for them to enter my territory: the only ones I have a real hold over are the northern chiefs…' The savage smell of the fires drifted past them, carried on the night air. 'We didn't only stop here to organise their defence against the Stiengs!'

The increasingly frequent rifle shots, like slow motion machine gun fire, nourished Perken's obsession: they appeared and disappeared, emphasising the constancy of the motionless fires. New fires were lit: as the rifle fire accelerated, they appeared, stationary, at various degrees of distance. Beneath the rapid flash of the rifles, their immobility was so solemn that it seemed indifferent to the fighting, as if born out of the heat and the night.

'Do you think they could join forces to mount an attack?' Claude asked.

'There are a lot of them now: look at the fires...' Perken reflected. 'They could certainly take the village. But they're quite incapable of joining forces. My men and the chiefs I was hoping to unite are all Laotian Buddhists, just like the people of this region, and it's almost impossible to hold them together. Add to that, the Stiengs always attack anyone passing through. It isn't easy to mount an attack when there are old corpses lying around, their smell makes it hard to prepare. The thing that's really driving them at the moment is starvation. Tomorrow, they'll have the militia on their heels again...' He reflected again. 'And so will we...'

The fusillade resumed and then again diminished, an arc against the fires. A man emerged from the shadows at the entrance to the hut, his bare feet as noiseless as hands on the rungs of the ladder. In the murky light of the lamp, the patch of brightness rose: head, chest, leg. A messenger. Perken lifted himself, grimaced with pain, and fell back again. When the pain increased, it was so dominant that, in order to give orders, he had to wait for it to lessen, like a living creature falling. The man was already speaking rapidly, in short phrases, in the tone of someone reciting. Claude guessed that he had learnt these Siamese phrases by heart, and he looked towards Perken, as if it was easier to understand a European's silence. Perken stopped looking at the man, who was still speaking, and closed his eyes: if it were not for the imperceptible quivering of his cheeks, he might have been asleep. Suddenly he looked up.

'What's the matter?' Claude asked.

'He says the Stiengs know I'm here and that's why they're attacking, why they keep coming back. Besides, we're less dangerous enemies than the militia…'

The fusillade stopped. The messenger left, accompanied by Xa.

'The village can't be surrounded… We have the rifles…'

Two shots rang out, followed by their echoes, then silence fell again.

'…He also says there are railway engineers with the militia…'

Claude was starting to understand. 'But they're hard at work over there! They detonate at least ten mines a day…'

'Each time they do, it feels like people screaming in my head… They're advancing, there's no doubt of that… If they come here…'

'Would they change their route now?'

Perken made no gesture. He lay motionless, looking at the shadow before him. 'It would save them a lot of money if they passed through my territory… You can see how brave they are: the Mois are fleeing like animals. They won't pass that way, even with the militia.'

Claude did not reply.

'…Even with the militia…' he repeated. He fell silent again. 'If we'd had three machine guns, just three machine guns, they would never have been able to get through…'

The fusillade started up again, weakly, then stopped.

'They'll be quiet now. It's almost daylight.'

'Is Savan supposed to be coming at sunrise?'

'I think so… Pack of idiots! If they let the militia in…'

3

Savan climbed the ladder. How many dawns still remained before the disaster? Perken watched as the man's close-cropped grey hair, his worried eyes, his nose like that of a Laotian Buddha, rose in the door frame. Since death had taken up residence in him, people had started to lose their shape. Although he knew this chief, he existed less to him, individually, than the old chief of the Stieng village. But his hands were ready for parley… This was a man who was good at speaking and not much else. Other heads appeared, one above the other: the men following him. They all entered. Savan hesitated: he did not like to crouch in front of white men, and hated sitting. He remained standing, eyes fixed on his feet, and said nothing. Everyone waited. This oriental silence exasperated Claude. Perken was used to it, but it had become more painful since he had been wounded: waiting made him intensely aware of his own immobility.

He made up his mind to speak first. 'If the militia come here, you know what will happen.'

There was enough light now to make out the vista of the slopes, receding to the horizon. A few hundred metres away, skulls attached to solitary trees emerged from the darkness. The dawn wind bent the treetops, and the great waves of vegetation, repeated from hill to hill, seemed to continue the movement, borne on the invisible flight of the tribes. A mine exploded. They could not see the area where they were laying the railway line, on the other side of the hut, but immediately after the rumbling that filled the valley, they heard the sound of stones and chunks of rock raining down.

'The militia will be here the day after tomorrow. As I've already said, if you resist, with the firearms you have, they'll go back up north. If you don't, the railway will pass through here. Do you want to be under the thumb of Siamese functionaries?'

Savan replied with a negative but suspicious gesture.

'It's easier to fight militiamen who don't have orders to attack you than to fight regular troops who've come via the railway…'

'I may be dead before then,' he said in French to Claude.

His tone was striking: he had started to believe again in his own life.

One by one, natives entered the hut, and crouched. They did not speak Siamese among themselves, and Perken did not understand their dialect, but it was clear that they were hostile. Savan pointed to them. 'It's the Stiengs they're most afraid of.'

'The Stiengs can't do anything against rifles!'

The chief's finger, which had remained in the air, now turned to the jungle. Perken picked up his binoculars and looked at the trees: at the tops of the tallest, poles rose one by one, surmounted by crude lumps: the Stiengs had stopped fleeing. For lack of enough fetishes, a whole world of skulls, of animals killed in hunting, emerged from the jungle, imprinted the threat of the savages on the morning sky, as if the *gaur*'s skull had given birth to an abundance of bones which were now moving down to the river, in flight themselves, insects swarming around them. Ribcages, skulls, even snakeskins swayed up there, as white as chalk, a sudden assertion of the starvation whose ravages were forcing the savages to migrate. To the right, towards the river, a haunting fetish representing a woman weeping over the dead, with a sorrow unknown to civilised people, surmounted with a human skull surrounded by small feathers. Perken lowered his binoculars. More natives were entering the hut. Two of them carried rifles, which glinted in the shadows: he remembered the hut where Grabot's jacket had hung.

'You're gambling with everyone's life. If you send mediators and shoot at the militiamen, they won't insist. I know the orders they have. And they can take the Stiengs from the rear. Otherwise…'

Some of those present could understand Siamese. He was interrupted by voices raised in vehement protest, like dogs barking.

Savan hesitated, then made up his mind to speak. 'They say it's your fault the Stiengs are attacking us.'

'They're attacking you because they're dying of starvation.'

Everyone, now, was looking at Savan, who hesitated again, but spoke at last. 'They say, without you, they would leave us alone.'

Perken shrugged.

'And they want you to go.'

Perken hit the boards with his fist. All the natives who had been crouching leapt to their feet like frogs. The two with rifles took aim at the white men.

'This is it,' Claude thought. 'How stupid!'

Perken looked beyond the line of threatening faces, but Xa was not in the hut. 'If they move,' he cried, as if looking at something behind the natives, 'fire!'

Without lowering their rifles, they turned as quickly as they could. Two gunshots rang out: Perken had fired through his pocket. The jolt was so painful that he thought for a second he had shot himself in the knee. One of the men toppled. The other had dropped his rifle and was standing, clutching his stomach with both hands, his mouth open, a stunned expression in his eyes like that of a dying man. The general flight caused him in turn to topple, one hand raised above the stampeding heads. Once the noise of bare feet receded, silence fell again.

Only Savan had remained. 'What now?' he said to Perken.

He was resigned now, awaiting the disasters which the madness of white men always brought with them sooner or later. The world of Buddhist detachment in which he lived seemed to surround him. Above the two huddled bodies, from which blood was flowing noiselessly, he stood staring into space, motionless as a ghost in front of the deserted clearing. 'Those who were shouting loudest just now must have been his rivals,' Perken thought. 'I don't think he's angry at being rid of them…' Suddenly he saw them there in front of him, the blood flowing out of them through invisible holes, as if out of something that had never been alive: although he had known they were there, he had had the impression they had fled with the others. They were dead. But what was he? Alive? Dying? How could he get Savan on his side? What did they have in common? Self-interest and fear, he knew. Yes, you could get these people to rise up, but only in the event of rebellion or war: things he had spent years waiting for. If Savan had agreed to fight against the militia, half the village would almost certainly have fled. These alliances, of which he had once had such expectations, even that they might give his life meaning, suddenly seemed to him as fragile as this hesitant Laotian with whom he had never fought. Against the invading white men, against the militia, against these mines that were shaking the valleys, the only men he could count on were those with whom he had a human connection, those who believed in loyalty: his own people. And even they… If he hadn't been wounded, these Laotians would never have dared train their rifles on him. He might be diminished in their eyes, but he wasn't yet diminished in the eyes of his own people: these two had just seen that. He looked up at Savan: their eyes met and he saw, as clearly if the chief had spoken, that to him he was a doomed man. For the second time, he saw his own death in another man's eyes. He had a strong desire to shoot him, as if murder were the only way to assert his existence, to struggle against his own end. He would see that look again in the eyes of his own men. That insane feeling that he could grab death by the throat and fight like an animal, which had gripped him when he had thought of shooting Savan, spread within him with the force of a seizure. He would fight his worst enemy, decay, in the soul of each of his men. He remembered one of his uncles, a Danish squire who, after a thousand follies, had had himself buried as the king of the Huns, sitting astride his dead horse held upright by poles, and who, during his death agony, had forced himself not to scream even once, although every fibre in his body was crying out for him to do so, to chase away the terror that made his shoulders shake like a St Vitus's Dance…

'I'm going up there…'

4

No more villages. Against the sky, the first of the mountains from which Perken was hoping for his deliverance. Below, the river. The reflections of birds and butterflies in heavy flight glided over the surface of the jungle, but ahead of the Mois, who were being driven as far as the horizon by the militia, the smaller animals, the monkeys in particular, were fleeing in panic, as if before a fire. They were crossing the river in their hundreds, arriving like eddies of leaves, and stopping on the bank with their tails in the air, like cats. A big monkey was moving about in the middle of the water, probably standing on a stone: through the binoculars, Claude could see him very distinctly, busy tearing off the little ones who were clinging to his back, like a wet dog shaking water from its fur. When they reached the other bank, they disappeared like a gust of wind amid the crackling of branches, and their flight from one part of the jungle to the other linked the dazzling river to the great exodus of the tribes.

The fires, alight all day now, spread a curtain of smoke over the slopes: even the intense noon light could not diminish it. It gradually advanced halfway down the mountains, towards the path the white men were following, even though there was not a breath of wind: a human advance, like the muffled stamping of an army. The smoke of each new fire, more menacing than the previous one because of its position, rose straight into the air in a dense plume, before it disintegrated and joined the curtain. Claude was looking a kilometre ahead, waiting anxiously for another column of smoke to rise, like someone waiting for a key to turn in a lock. 'That one will be a fire soon. One more, and we won't be able to get through.'

Perken's eyes were closed all the time now. 'There are moments when I feel as if none of this matters,' he said between his teeth, as if talking to himself.

'Being cut off?'

'No: death.'

Beyond the mountains, Perken's territory, protected by them, crushed beneath the solitary ridges where no fires burnt. On the other side, the railway. If Perken died, Claude would get back to the bas-reliefs, which were waiting for him. The Stiengs would never dare attack the line on their own.

Perken was sinking into a stupor. Very close to his ears, mosquitoes buzzed softly. The pain of the bites was transparent, covering the pain of his wound like filigree. It, too, rose and fell, inflaming the fever, forcing Perken into a nightmarish struggle not to touch himself – as if the other pain were lying in wait for him, with this one as a decoy. He was startled by a fleshly sound: it was his own fingers, mesmerised by the insect bites, drumming convulsively on the cart without his realising it. Everything he had thought about life was decomposing beneath the fever like a body in the earth. A sudden jolt, stronger than most, brought him back to the surface of life. Returning at that moment, pulled into consciousness by Claude's words and the forward momentum of the cart, which he could not separate one from the other, he felt so weak that he did not recognise his own sensations, and this intolerable awakening both threw him back into a life he was trying to flee and into his own person, which he would have liked to find again. If only he could apply his mind to something! He tried to lift himself to look at the new fire, but before he could move, a mine exploded, far ahead of him. The earth fell back, lifelessly. The Mois' dogs started howling.

'The only thing that matters is the militia, Claude. As long as the railway hasn't been finished, we can get to them. We'd have to cut off their communications in the rear, isolate the front of the line, seize their weapons… It isn't impossible… Provided I get there! Damned fever… When this is over, I'd at least like… Claude?'

'Yes, I'm listening.'

'My death should at least force them to be free.'

'What difference would it make to you?'

Perken had closed his eyes: impossible to make himself understood by a living man.

'Does it hurt again?'

'Only when there's a bad jolt. But I'm too weak. It's not natural… It'll start again.'

He looked at the mountaintops, then at the hill where the mine had just exploded. To keep his binoculars still, he had to lean on the wood of the cart. His head lolled from side to side. At last, he stopped it moving.

'I wouldn't even be able to shoot now…'

Up there, the bullocks were bringing sleepers, which the Siamese tipped over, and setting off again with the efficiency of machines, turning around the last one like Grabot in his hut. Every time a sleeper fell without the slightest sound, as if in another world, he felt the echo in his knee. That line, advancing like a battering ram towards the mountains on the horizon, would not only pass over his hopes, but over his actual corpse, his decaying eyes, his ears eaten away by the earth. Although the sound of the wood falling did not reach him, he heard it, moment by moment, in the throbbing of his blood. He knew he would get better once he was back in his own territory, and at the same time he knew that he was going to die, that the world would close over the cluster of hopes that had constituted his life, with this railway line as the finishing touch, like a noose around a prisoner's neck. He knew that nothing in the universe would ever be able to compensate for his sufferings, present or past: to be a man was even more absurd than to be dying... More and more numerous, huge and vertical in the blaze of noon, the columns of smoke from the Mois' fires covered the horizon like a gigantic grille. Everything – the heat, the fever, the cart, the burning sensations, the barking dogs, the sleepers flung down like shovelfuls of earth being thrown onto his body, the grille of smoke, the power of the jungle, death itself – merged in one superhuman sense of imprisonment, all hope gone. Beyond the singing of the mosquitoes, the dogs were howling now from one end of the valley to the other. Others answered, behind the hills. The cries filled the jungle as far as the horizon, crowding the empty spaces between the columns of smoke. He was a prisoner, still trapped in the world of men as if in an underground tunnel, with these threats, these fires, this absurdity lurking around him like animals dwelling in cellars. Beside him, Claude, Claude who was going to live, who believed in life as others believed that the men who were torturing them were human: an odious belief. Alone. Alone with the fever that went through him from his head to his knee, and that loyal thing placed on his thigh: his hand.

For some days, he had been seeing it like this: free, separate from him. It lay there on his thigh, looking at him calmly, accompanying him to that lonely region into which he was sinking, with the sensation that his body was submerged in hot water. He came back to the surface for a moment, recalled that hands tensed when the death agony began. He was sure of that. In this flight towards a world as elemental as that of the jungle, a dreadful awareness remained: the hand was there, white, fascinating, the fingers above the heavy palm, the nails clutching the threads of his shorts like spiders hanging from their webs by the ends of their legs above the hot leaves. There it was, in front of him, in the formless world in which he was struggling, just as the other men struggled in the clammy depths of the jungle. Not enormous: simple, natural, but alive, like an eye. That was death.

Claude was looking at him: the howling of the wild dogs went well with this ravaged, unshaven face, eyelids lowered, sleeping with a sleep so absent it could only express the approach of death. The only man who had loved him for what he was, and what he wanted to be, not what he'd been as a child… He did not dare touch him. But his head knocked against the wood of the cart: Claude lifted it, and pushed back the helmet to wedge it, leaving the forehead clear. Perken opened his eyes: the sky rushed in, overpowering and yet full of joy. A few branches without insects passed between the sky and him, shimmering like the air, like the last Laotian woman he had possessed. He knew nothing of men now, nothing even of the earth moving beneath him with its trees and its animals. All he knew was this vastness, white because of the light, this tragic joy into which he was being swallowed, and which was gradually filled with the muffled beating of his heart.

All he could hear now was himself, as if he alone could match the blazing heat that was tearing his soul from the jungle, as if he alone could express the obsessive response of his wound to the sacred sky. 'It seems to me I'm gambling everything on the hour of my death…' Life was there, in the dazzling light which was swallowing the earth. *The other* was there, too, in the obsessive hammering of his veins. But there was no struggle between them: this heart would stop beating, would also be swallowed in the implacable summons of the light… His hand had ceased to exist, his body had ceased to exist, there was only the pain: what did the word 'decay' mean? His eyes were burning, his eyelids like shutters. A mosquito landed on one of them: he could no longer move. Claude wedged his head with the tent canvas, and put his helmet back on top of his head. The shade made him withdraw back into himself.

He saw himself as he had once been, falling in a river, drunk, singing at the top of his voice above the lapping of the water. Now, too, death was around him, stretching to the horizon like the quivering air. Nothing would ever give his life meaning, not even this elation which was throwing him into the jaws of the sun. There were men on earth who believed in their own passions and sorrows, in their own existence: they were like insects under leaves, multitudes beneath the vault of death. It filled him with a deep joy, which echoed in his chest and in his leg at each throb of his blood in his wrists, temples and heart: it hammered home the madness of a world swallowed by the sun. And yet no man had ever died, ever: they had passed, like the clouds that had earlier become absorbed into the sky, like the jungle, like the temples. He alone was going to die, to be torn from this place.

His hand came back to life. It was motionless, but he could feel it, could feel the blood flowing out of it, could hear its liquid sound that merged with the sound of the river. His memories were there, waiting, held back by those menacing, half-tensed fingers. Like the movement of the fingers, the invasion of memories would herald the end. They would crowd in on him as he lay dying, as dense as the columns of smoke which came with the distant sound of tam-tams and the barking of the dogs. He clenched his teeth, longing to escape his own body and not abandon the incandescent sky which had seized him like an animal: a horrible pain, like the pain of a limb being torn off, swept over him from his knee to his head. He was in a tunnel, somewhere deep beneath the earth, a tunnel about to collapse… He bit his lip so hard that the blood started running.

Claude saw the blood welling between his teeth. But the pain was protecting his friend against death: as long as he suffered, he was alive. Suddenly, he imagined himself in Perken's place: never had he been so attached to this life he didn't even like. The blood was flowing in rivulets over Perken's chin, like the blood that had emerged from the bullet in the *gaur*'s skull, and there was nothing he could do but look at those red teeth biting, and wait.

'If I remember right,' Perken was thinking, 'I'm going to die…' His whole life was around him, terrifying and patient, like the Stiengs surrounding the hut… 'Maybe we don't remember after all…' He dreaded his past as much as his hand. Yet, despite his will and his pain, he saw himself again throwing away his Colt and walking towards the Stiengs in the slanting light of evening. But that couldn't herald his death: that was another man, in a previous life. When he got back to his own territory, what would he do against these mines that were pounding his fevered brain? The pain returned, and he knew that he would never get back to his territory, as if he had learnt it from the salty taste of his own blood: in his pain, he tore at the skin on his chin, his teeth scrubbed by his stiff beard. The pain was rousing him again, but if it became any more intense, it would drive him mad, he would be like a woman in labour screaming for it to be over – men were still being born into this world… It wasn't his youth that was coming back to him, as he had expected, but the dead, as if death itself had summoned them… 'I don't want to be buried alive!' But the hand was there, with its burden of memories, like the eyes of the savages the other night in the darkness: he wouldn't be buried alive.

'Imperceptibly,' Claude thought, 'the face has stopped being human.' His shoulders tensed. The anguish seemed unchanging, like the sky above the dogs' funereal lamentation, which was fading now into the dazzling silence. He was face to face with the vanity of being a man, sick with silence and the implacable indictment of the world constituted by the death of someone you loved. More powerful than the jungle or the sky, death seized his face and forced it to turn towards its eternal combat. 'How many people, at this hour, are watching over bodies like this?' Almost all these bodies, lost in the night of Europe or the daylight of Asia, also crushed by the futility of their lives, and full of hatred for those who would wake up in the morning and console themselves with gods. Oh, if only the gods existed, so that, even if it meant eternal pain, you could howl like those dogs, howl that no thoughts of heaven, no future reward, nothing could justify the end of a human existence, to escape the futility of howling it in the total calm of the day, to escape from those closed eyes, those bloodstained teeth still tearing the skin to shreds!… To escape that ravaged head, that monstrous defeat!

The lips half opened. 'There is no… death… There is only… *me*…' A finger tensed on the thigh. '*Me… about to die…*'

Claude remembered, with hatred, a phrase he had learnt as a child: 'Lord be with us in the hour of our death…' If only he could express through hands and eyes, or even through words, that desperate sense of fraternity which was thrusting him beyond his own limits! He gripped him by the shoulders.

Perken was looking at this witness, as foreign to him now as a creature from another world.

Notes

1. Shelter for travellers (*Malraux's note*).
2. Aurochs from southern Asia (*Malraux's note*).
3. The loyalty oath consists of drinking from the same jar. Jars are the most precious objects in Stieng villages (*Malraux's note*).
4. Screen suspended from a ceiling used as a ventilator, operated by pulling on ropes attached to it.

Biographical note

André Malraux was born in Paris in 1901. His parents divorced in 1905, and he was brought up by his mother, a shopkeeper on the outskirts of Paris, and his grandmother. He rarely saw his father, who committed suicide in 1930, and from an early age sought escape in books and museums. After abandoning his studies and working for booksellers and publishers, he married his first wife Clara Goldschmidt in 1921. He embarked with her on his first voyage to French Indochina in 1923. There he was arrested for stealing bas-reliefs from temples in Banteay Srei, and narrowly avoided a three-year prison sentence thanks to a petition signed by some of France's leading intellectuals. He briefly returned to Indochina in 1925, where he founded anti-colonial newspapers, which were eventually closed down by the authorities, and joined the revolutionary Young Annam League.

Malraux's life of adventure, military exploits and political activism saw him gain considerable recognition and influence as a public figure. Some claimed he exaggerated his achievements – he was involved in revolutionary activities in China, fought for the Republican cause in the Spanish Civil War and joined the French Resistance. This reputation was further enhanced by his novels – including *The Temptation of the West* (1926), *The Conquerors* (1928), *The Way of the Kings* (1930), the Prix Goncourt-winning *Man's Fate* (1933) and *Man's Hope* (1937). Under the two governments of Charles de Gaulle – who would remain a lifelong friend of his – he was Minister of Information (1945-46) and Minister of Cultural Affairs (1958-69). During this second mandate Malraux's profile was raised even further as he undertook substantial projects which included extensive, and at times controversial, renovations of monuments and the creation of cultural centres, major exhibitions and a national inventory. He was also a keen cultural ambassador for his country, meeting the likes of Mao and Nehru. Among intellectual circles he was at times criticised for his unwavering support of de Gaulle and his policies, particularly in regard to the Algerian War.

Throughout his life he wrote countless essays and articles and was renowned for his energetic and impassioned speeches. Apart from his novels, his major works include the writings on art collected in *The Psychology of Art* (1947–8), and his *Anti-Memoirs* (1967-76), part fiction, part autobiography. Malraux died in 1976 of a pulmonary embolism after several years of ill health. His ashes were transferred to the Panthéon in 1996.

Howard Curtis lives and works in London. He has translated many works of fiction and non-fiction. His translation of Edoardo Albinati's *Coming Back*, published by Hesperus Press, won the 2004 John Florio Prize for Italian Translation.

SELECTED TITLES FROM HESPERUS PRESS

Author	Title	Foreword writer
Mikhail Bulgakov	*A Dog's Heart*	A.S. Byatt
Mikhail Bulgakov	*The Fatal Eggs*	Doris Lessing
F. Scott Fitzgerald	*The Popular Girl*	Helen Dunmore
F. Scott Fitzgerald	*The Rich Boy*	John Updike
Franz Kafka	*Metamorphosis*	Martin Jarvis
Franz Kafka	*The Trial*	Zadie Smith
Carlo Levi	*Words are Stones*	Anita Desai
Katherine Mansfield	*In a German Pension*	Linda Grant
Katherine Mansfield	*Prelude*	William Boyd
Vladimir Mayakovsky	*My Discovery of America*	Colum McCann
Luigi Pirandello	*Loveless Love*	
Jean-Paul Sartre	*The Wall*	Justin Cartwright